BONE ISLAND

BONE ISLAND

CHRIS MCPHERSON

Ekstasis Editions

National Library of Canada Cataloguing in Publication Data

McPherson, Christopher
Bone Island

ISBN 1-894800-13-3

I. Title.
PS8575.P47B66 2002   C813'.54   C2002-910744-X
PR9199.3.M42483B66 2002

Cover Design:
Author Photo: Bonnie Secret

Acknowledgments:
Lyrics on pages 115 quoted by permission. ©1968 Robin Williamson.
Published by Warner-Tamarlanne Music Corp. (BMI)
The author wishes to thank both the Canada Council and the British
Columbia Arts Council for support during the writing of this novel.

Published in 2002 by:
Ekstasis Editions Canada Ltd.   Ekstasis Editions
Box 8474, Main Postal Outlet   Box 571
Victoria, B.C. V8W 3S1   Banff, Alberta ToL oCo

BoneIsland has been published with the assistance of a grant from the Canada
Council for the Arts and the Cultural Services Branch of British Columbia.

for my dad...

and for Bonnie...

Adam and Sylvie are making love in the basement. They probably think I'm asleep, and I should be. I've got the plans for the renovations to my sister's husband's warehouse spread out all over the floor. For maybe the last half hour I've been sitting here staring out at the darkness like I expect to see a ghost.

I may have dozed, but now I'm sure I'm wide awake—acutely aware of the murmurous ululations of my son and his girlfriend just under my feet. I'm wondering with half a mind what I *should* be feeling—and maybe with the other half I'm wondering what I *am* feeling—when my father's ghost comes tramping up the steps onto the porch and peers in the window.

My father, Homer Knee, is a large man, but I can see right through him. His beard—long-grizzled—has gone white as snow. He carries his old rain-stained leather briefcase, wears his yellow slicker and gumboots, though the August night is warm and clear. Over his shoulder, Perseid meteors etch the night. I let him in.

Bonnie is on night-shift at Osburn's—she won't be home for hours. Speed Avenue is quiet, sulking in shadow. Homer smells of the sea. Haven't seen him this far inland for years.

Cup of tea, maybe? he says.

I make it strong, the way he likes it. But when I bring the pot in from the kitchen—he is gone. A faint odor of kelp lingers, or maybe I'm imagining it. I stand for a long time, listening, but the house is silent.

October afternoon. Last night's rain brought down more leaves from the big plane trees on Speed Avenue. The phone is ringing as I come up the steps.

It is Katherine's friend Kate. Bad news, Larry. It's your old man—he's dead. Kathy went up there and she found him.

How is she?

She's freaked, man. Frankly, I don't know how she made it back here. He'd been like—dead for a while. Know what I mean? Not much left of him. I guess the ravens and the shithawks had been at him.

Katherine worked for Homer the last couple of years he ran his bookstore. When he moved out to Bone Island the last time, she took over the store. She was my father's friend—his agent, his business manager, and lately his only link to the civilized world. She visited Homer every couple of months, braving the logging roads with her kayak lashed on top of Homer's old white Toyota, bringing him his mail and news and books. She stayed the night, sometimes longer.

Not this time.

You okay, Larry?

Sure.

You want me to call your sister?

I'll call her. Is Katherine going to be okay?

She'll live. I gave her a couple of downers and put her to bed. It must have been pretty gross. She got there and the place was

8

deserted. Then she spotted the birds out on the point. He'd been lying there for a long time, Larry—weeks—maybe months, but Kathy couldn't bring herself to go off and leave him there like that. She got a blanket to cover him up—but I guess some of the birds were still at him so she wrapped his bones up in the blanket and dragged them back up to the shack. You'd better phone the Mounties—I've got the number. Kathy called them and they sent a boat out to get him. What was left.

I look at the clock. It is only a quarter past five and my father is dead. I dial my sister's number, get Duncan.

Chief. How's it going?

Okay. Leila's not home yet I guess?

Not yet. Listen, chief—a couple of things I remembered I wanted to talk to you about. Those revisions—

My father has been lying on the beach feeding the sea gulls for a month, and right at the moment I can't get very excited about the flashing detail on your fucking parapet walls, chief, I say, or maybe I only think of saying it. More likely I mumble something about getting Leila to call me. It is only sixteen minutes past five and things are coming apart.

Bonnie gets her break at five-thirty. There's no women's washroom on the shop floor so she has to walk all the way up to the office to have a pee and wash up. By the time she calls at five thirty-seven, I've talked to Corporal Desh of the Royal Mounted—had a drink of water—taken my boots off. I've got a handle on it.

What's wrong, Larry? she says, after I say hello. Maybe I don't have a handle on it.

It's Homer. Katherine found him. He's dead.

Christ. Is she okay?

Kate gave her some pills. It was Kate who called me. He died on the beach, Bonnie, out on the point.

That's cool.

For *him*, maybe. Not so cool for Katherine. He'd been out there for a while.

Shit. I see what you mean. Jesus. Are you okay, Larry? I'll tell John I've got a family emergency. I'll be home in ten minutes.

Hey, I'm okay. Don't panic. I thought you said this week was the beginning of the big crunch. If they need you there—

Of course they need me. Do *you* need me, Larry?

Of course I do. But I really am fine. Just rerunning a bunch of old footage, you know—wondering when the feelings are going to kick in. Don't ruin John's night on account of me.

Jesus, Larry. Do they have any idea what he died of?

I phoned the Mounties. Katherine called them and they sent a boat out to get him. They figure he'd been out there a month at least. He was *naked*, Bonnie. Not a scrap of clothing anywhere near the body. Just an empty whiskey bottle. He'd been sober almost five years.

Shit. Didn't you have some dream that he'd died? I remember you telling me something about a dream…

In the summer. I dreamt his ghost came to visit me. At least I *thought* it was a dream—he had his rain gear on. He didn't stay for tea. The Mountie wanted to know if I knew the name of his dentist.

To identify him?

I guess the turkey vultures and other scavengers really did a job on him. Picked him pretty clean. Katherine dragged him all the way back up to the house. *You've* been there, Bonnie. Shit, it must be a hundred and fifty yards—if he was right out on the point. That was his favourite spot, under that old blasted pine.

10

Homer was a big guy. Katherine's maybe five-one on a tall day. She couldn't have dragged Homer *down* that hill, with all the flesh on him.

I'll tell John I've got to go home.

I'll pick you up. You can throw your bike in the truck.

Before I make it out the door, the phone is ringing again. I know it is my sister Leila, but I answer it.

Hey, Larry.

Leila.

Duncan said you called.

Homer's dead.

We listen to our hearts push blood through our ears. When…What…How?

Katherine found him. Kate called me. It wasn't pretty. The Mounties figure he drank himself insensible—died of exposure. An empty whiskey bottle beside the body. You don't happen to know if he ever went to the dentist, do you?

The dentist? God, I don't know—not since that Doctor what's-his-name—Pittman or something—that we all went to. He died years ago. What's this about a bottle? I thought he'd been sober for—God—it's been years, hasn't it?

Five years. I don't know, Leila; I've been thinking about it—maybe it was suicide. He hadn't had a drink in five years. He was out there naked on the point. Maybe he wasn't sure the alcohol would be enough to kill him—but he figured the cold would finish the job. The Mounties didn't find a note or anything. If Katherine found anything she didn't tell them. They'll probably rule it accidental. Listen—I've got to pick up Bonnie.

Did you say *naked*?

Apparently.

Oh God, I just got it, the dentist is because—Oh God, so like what you've been trying to tell me is we won't be having an open casket?

It was pretty rough on Katherine, I say.

Good thing she's a tough little number. *She* should know if he's got a dentist.

Apparently not. Listen, I've got—

Hey, what about his war wound? He had that piece of shrapnel in his knee, right? They *did* find his *knees*, didn't they?

Bonnie's waiting with her bike on the loading dock.

Was John pissed off?

He didn't kiss me.

I will then.

Not here. Give me the keys. I'll drive.

I haven't had a drink.

I didn't say you had.

I give her the keys. We don't speak again till we are parked in the fallen leaves on Speed Avenue.

Okay, she says.

She holds me and I cry.

Later, in bed, Bonnie says, It's funny about the ghost.

What?

Somebody—I think it was Ambrose Bierce—said all ghosts should be naked.

Ambrose Bierce? I say. Before she hitchhiked into my life—and long long before she decided to train as a machinist—Bonnie did a degree in North American Lit at the University of Saskatchewan.

12

The writer, she says. He didn't believe in the resurrection of textiles or whatever. But when you saw Homer's ghost he had his rain gear on. Even though he was stark naked when he died.

It was a dream, I say.

Well, then—even more so.

How have I come so far from where? Is this person really me, who always had a father, but doesn't, anymore? Always had a prickly-chinned large presence of a dad. Who is this suddenly fatherless person pretending to be me?

I don't get it. Might as well come to grips. All is lost, in the end. But I bridle at the night.

I think Bonnie is asleep, but she's bridling too. I can't see Homer killing himself and not leaving a note, she says, out of the darkness. Unless maybe that was the whole point. Like if he could've said it in a note he wouldn't have had to kill himself. Like maybe after spending his whole life trying to write it down—he finally realized he never could. I mean—when you think about it— a suicide note is kind of insult to injury, anyway. I mean what can you say? Sorry? Sorry doesn't fucking cut it, does it? I mean, like if you were *really* sorry—if you really cared about *anybody*—I mean the message is pretty clear, isn't it? A downer, maybe, but…

Who are these two people, in love for twenty years, both feeling right through to the bone in this dark moment, who lie and pretend to each other to be strong—these brave, these heart-less creatures?

I should sleep, I say.

You aren't going to work tomorrow? she says.

I got block-layers coming.

Let Tim and Duncan deal with them. Jesus Christ—you don't think they expect you to…

I'll take some time off, but I'll have to arrange it. I want to go talk to Katherine.

You think he *did* leave a note, don't you?

I don't know. But there's going to be arrangements—legal shit. If he left any instructions or a will or anything he probably left it with her.

You don't suppose he was worth anything, do you? I mean all he had was the book store and that old white car and he gave them both to her already.

I don't know. I just can't believe he's never going to be alive again.

He used to come visit me, you know. When Adam was little—when you took those jobs up-island, to try and finish your apprenticeship. He used to come by late at night—pissed and horny. Adam would be asleep, but I'd be up late reading and he'd come tramping up the steps and I'd make him tea and fend him off and send him home.

You never told me.

He meant no harm. It was all a game. But I knew how you'd take it. You already hated him for betraying your mother. He would have died rather than hurt you.

Right. That's why he was getting plastered and coming on to my wife while his grandson slept in the next room and I was up in Port Hardy, framing twelve hours a day in the rain and sharing a moldy motel room with a three hundred pound labourer who snored like the last train out of hell.

It was just a game, Larry. Homer liked to play games. One time I called his bluff. When he got fresh—I didn't fend him off. Just for fun, I encouraged him instead—responded to his advances. He was gone before the water boiled, that time, too.

I can believe that. But what would you have done if he hadn't bolted?

14

What if is a country I don't visit, Larry, she says. You know that.

Next morning early. I wake and smother my alarm clock a moment before it goes off. Bonnie sleeps sprawled like a cat—I leave her dreaming. I sit in the glow of the stove-top light and squeeze my coffee cup and look at the phone, but I don't call my mother in New York. It is raining again; I can hear it rattle on the fiberglass panels of the greenhouse roof.

No sign of morning light as I warm up my truck. I sit in the throbbing cab and chew a dry shredded wheat biscuit right out of the packet. At the other end of Speed Avenue—the dead end—a taxi waits, parking lights on, motor running.

Sometimes I see reflections approaching, in the glass of the Mayfair Motel across Speed Avenue. They never round the corner. Sometimes I see reflections leaving, but they were never here. Speed Avenue is exactly one block long. When we moved here there were still bikers living in the big white house. After the last of them headed north to Nanaimo, a bunch of ecofreaks took over the place. Sometimes I imagine a place where time melts and the two groups fuse. In my mind, Speed Avenue roars with the Harleys of a band of ecobikers—big men and women with old growth tattoos on their brawny forearms—roaring off to spike the Clayoquot and raise a little politically incorrect hell.

Tim has opened the gate in the hoarding. I pull in beside his truck. Tim's drinking coffee from a styrofoam cup, talking with the plumber.

No block-layer?

I ain't seen any block-layers—what about you, Norm?

15

The plumber grins and chews. He's eating an apple.

Hey, says Tim, ain't this a union holiday?

Naw, says Norm, checking his watch. We'll hear him on his motorbike at one minute to eight—you wait.

Maybe ten minutes after, says Tim.

I pull up a sawhorse, open my thermos. Sylvie comes in, singing softly to herself, pushing her bike. Sylvie drove one of those pedicabs for the tourists all summer—she thinks construction labouring is a piece of cake. Adam is back at school on the mainland. Have to call and tell him about Homer.

Who else? Who should know? Such a private man, Homer. Did he have any friends? Besides Katherine and maybe Margaret, the Nuu-chah-nulth elder who was his only neighbor on that lonely coast. What about from before? He had a few drinking buddies in the old days, but they are probably all dead, or should be.

Randy, the block-layer, pulls into the yard on his Harley—the unmistakable hiccupping rhythm of the machine suddenly huge and hollow on the drum of the hoarding. One minute to eight. I screw the lid back on my thermos. Duncan sticks his head around the door of his temporary office.

How you doing, chief? Listen, could you—

I can hear Leila's voice through the door, and Duncan's head disappears, then reappears, then is gone again, like a puppet. I shrug, go outside to show Randy what needs to be done.

When I climb down off the scaffolding, a few minutes later, Leila is waiting at the bottom. Nice tattoos, she says, her eyebrows indicating Randy, up above. He's hung his leather jacket off a scaffold brace, works in a sleeveless shirt in spite of the season. Where do you find these guys, Larry?

You keep your mitts off him till he's finished that parapet wall, I say.

I don't go for guys with ponytails, she says, eyeing mine. Listen, Larry—I called Mother this morning. I spared her the gory details. She wants to come out for the funeral.

You're kidding.

No. She wanted to know when it's going to be. Have you talked to Katherine yet?

I was just going to call her.

Mother also asked me about the book.

What book?

That's what I said. Mother said he only ever got suicidal when he'd just finished a book. And it only stands to reason. I mean what else was he doing out on that godforsaken rock?

I don't know. I thought he quit writing when he quit drinking. Katherine will know.

Kind of pathetic, isn't it? How little we know about our own father?

Homer was a very secretive guy.

Yeah, I know. But maybe—

Larry—Duncan at the door again. Phone for you, chief. It's Katherine.

I've got to go to work, says Leila. Ask her about the book.

Larry, says Katherine, sounding like a very small person speaking far away in a very large room. I take it you've got the book.

Me? I didn't even know there *was* a book.

Is your whole family a bunch of liars?

Probably. But I don't know anything about a book.

If you don't have it—who does? Not your sister.

Maybe he really did despair, Katherine. Maybe he threw it in the ocean.

Larry—if he wanted you to have it, he had his reasons. I just

17

don't see why you have to lie to me. Did he tell you to lie to me?

Are you at the bookstore?

Where else would I be?

Look—can I come over?

If you want. I thought I could trust *you*, Larry.

I'm not sure why I have to go talk to her. Maybe it's Duncan at his desk, pretending indifference. Maybe I'm hoping that if I look her in the eye she'll believe me, but on the way over I wonder if I'll be able to do it. I've been told I'm a bad liar—and that was when I was trying to tell the truth.

Before Homer bought the bookstore, it was called Used Books. Homer changed the name to Esoterica but he never got around to changing the sign. When he took over the place we all thought it would be an ideal occupation for him—a man who knew and loved books. But he never made much of a go of it. He loved seeking out and acquiring books, but he hated to part with them. I've been told buying a book from him was like trying to adopt a child.

Homer and my mother were still living together—or at least sharing a house—when he took the store over, but it wasn't long before he moved out and into the bookstore. He lived there for years, until he finally left Katherine in charge and moved out to Bone Island. He had a mattress in the cramped windowless attic, cooked on a hot-plate, though not often. Mostly he lived on whiskey and coffee and cigarettes, maybe a bit of brown bread, hard cheese and fruit. Sometimes he went down to Fisherman's Wharf to buy fresh fish, got pissed with the fishers and staggered home singing sea shanties. Next day he'd fry a piece of halibut on his hot-plate. The bookstore would smell of fish for days.

Katherine came to work for him the year before he quit

18

drinking. I think she was about nineteen at the time, the same age Adam is now. I don't know if Katherine was the *reason* Homer finally quit drinking, but I know he couldn't have done it without her. She never hid from him the fact that even then she was already living with an older woman.

Katherine sits in the window of the bookstore in Homer's big leather wing-back chair. Now—three years after he left her in charge—she seems to be making a go of the business. She sits watching the rain, a book open in her lap. She looks tiny in my father's chair. I've never seen her look so human. Usually she surrounds herself with an energy and a confidence which can intimidate, but today she is still and sad.

I move a pile of books, sit on the broad window sill, between her eyes and the rain. The rain continues on Discovery Street behind me, but her eyes drop to the book in her lap.

Are you okay? I say.

I'm sorry I called you a liar on the phone, Larry.

I'm sorry you had to go through this, I say.

Suddenly she meets my eyes.

I just can't believe he'd destroy it, she says. It meant *everything* to him. You have no idea. None of you had any idea.

She's right and I turn away. The book he was working on *always* meant everything to him, I say. Until he finished it. After that it was just flotsam—like all the others. I haven't often been close to my father, but I've known him a long time.

Have you? Did you really *know* him? Really? Ever? I'm beginning to wonder if *I* ever did. You think he did it on purpose, don't you?

I don't know. The Mounties said they found a whiskey bottle. If he hadn't had a drink in five years and he downed the whole thing—he must have had a pretty good idea what would happen.

I didn't bring it to him, Larry. I thought maybe he bought it when he brought you the book. *You* were the one he trusted. The only one, I think. Did you know that? He had his reasons not to trust *me*. But it was what kept me going—after I found him—thinking the manuscript must be safe with you. Now I don't know what to think.

My mother wants to come out for the funeral.

Jesus. Why? They've been divorced forever. She doesn't even send him a Christmas card.

Don't ask me. She's been asking about this book, too. She always liked his stuff.

So did I, says Katherine. Even if a lot of it *was* pretentious, obscure and self-indulgent—as he said himself. But when he was *on* he got me every time. And this time he was on. I know it—though of course the bastard never let me read a word of it. But he'd put it all together; you could see it in his eyes. This was the book he knew he couldn't write till he got sober, Larry, and I know what he went through to get sober. Do you?

We make eye contact once more.

We should have a real bloody Irish wake for him, says Katherine. A case of whiskey and an open casket. Let the rest of you have a look. I'm working on an obituary for the *Times-Colonist*. They'll cut it.

A customer enters.

I should get back to the job, I say.

Listen, Larry, I know he trusted you. You were the only one. So—if he told you to lie to me—I understand.

I *do* go back to the job, but I stop in at Speed Avenue on my way to see if Bonnie is awake. She is, though she doesn't look very happy about it. She's sitting at the kitchen table, peering out from behind her hair and a cup of coffee.

Corporal Desh of the Royal Mounted called, she says. They've been checking with dental clinics. Homer had a molar pulled last spring in Alberni—they're checking the X-rays. Did you talk to Katherine?

Yes. I just came from the bookstore. Shit.

What?

I totally spaced out and forgot to ask her if there was a will or anything.

Call her.

I will. She was all over me about the book Homer was writing. It's missing—she thinks I've got it. I didn't even know he was writing another book.

Of course he was.

I guess so. But where is it, then? I don't know, Bonnie—I guess I'd hoped he'd gotten over it. Like the drinking. I liked to think of him out there on the rocks with his casting rod and his binoculars—experiencing the last of his life with his mind unclouded by alcohol *or* literary ambition.

When I get back to the job site, Randy is gone and Sylvie has swept up his mess. Tim has a ledger bolted onto the block wall and he is starting to frame up the mezzanine. Sylvie carrying lumber for him and helping him lift the joists. Duncan must have told them about Homer. Nobody says anything—but I can tell by the way they look at me. I should put my tools on and give them a hand, but I don't. I tell Tim to call me at home if anything comes up.

I swing by Revelstoke Home Centre and pick out some nice clear cedar, put it on account. I take a slightly shame-faced pleasure in writing the warehouse address on the invoice, knowing Duncan will pick it up when he checks the receipts, but he won't have the balls to say anything.

I go home. Bonnie is in the greenhouse, reading Proust. I go downstairs to my shop and build a box. Homer always loved the smell of cedar.

My mother calls from New York.

How you doing, Larry?

Okay.

You sound out of breath.

I just ran up the stairs to get the phone. I thought it might be Tim calling from the job. I left him in charge.

Leila said you think Homer killed himself.

I don't know. He didn't leave a note and the book he was supposedly writing is nowhere to be found.

That woman has it.

Katherine? She thinks *I've* got it.

Obvious. Trying to divert your suspicions. I always knew she was ambitious. She probably plans to wait a year or two and publish it under her own name. You won't let her get away with it, Larry? You mustn't.

Jesus Christ, Mother. Homer wrote a slew of books in his life. Nobody ever offered him a dime for any of them. Are you trying to tell me that somebody would murder him for a *manuscript?*

I didn't say she killed him for it—I don't see the moral courage for murder in her. Probably she found him dead, just as she says. But I bet you she found the book, too, and she stole it.

It just doesn't make any sense. If he was a famous writer—even a moderately well-known writer—maybe…

Don't underestimate your father, Larry. He was a brilliant man. Lazy, moody, insensitive, hypocritical, and self-indulgent—but brilliant. I always knew that if he could transcend himself just a little…

Shit, Mother. Maybe he transcended himself a whole lot and threw the damn thing into the ocean. Then downed his first bottle in five years and lay down and died.

What does Bonnie think? She's always had more sense than you.

Bonnie thinks ghosts should be naked and suicide is a clear message.

Well—give her my love, anyway. I do want to fly out for the funeral. Are you having one? Did he leave instructions? Have you talked to his lawyer?

I didn't even know he *had* a lawyer.

Well, why should you? He never sued *you*. I believe you'll find he's still using that young woman he hired when he divorced me. She won't be such a young woman any more, I suppose. Olive something or other. Olive Ashcan—Ashtrakan—something like that. Try the phone book. There can't be many lawyers named Olive in a little place like that. Gotta go, honey. Call me as soon as you know anything. I'll bet you a frozen yogurt that woman has the book. Bye.

Her name is Olivia Astrakhan and she has an office on Fort Street. She's in a meeting when I call, but I barely have time to reset the table saw before she calls me back.

I sit down and catch my breath before I pick up the receiver.

Mr. Knee?

Speaking.

Olivia Astrakhan here. I hope nothing has happened to your

father?

I'm afraid so. He's dead.

Oh dear. Was it sudden?

Apparently. Unfortunately he was out there quite a while before he was found.

Oh dear. I did worry when he told me he was moving out there for good—a man of his age—no access to medical services. I suppose you're wondering about the will?

Did he leave any instructions? You know—cremation, burial, funeral services, that sort of thing? It's not something he ever talked about with us.

I don't think it concerned him. Once, when I asked him about it, he laughed and said, *Just leave me on the beach for the shorebirds.* We didn't put that in the will.

Well, I say, the shorebirds have had their share. The Mounties have what's left and I'm driving out day after tomorrow to sign the papers. I guess we'll get him cremated. Homer always loved a good hot fire.

I wish my father wasn't dead, that I was only driving out to the edge of the world to visit him on his rock, to chew on his smoked fish and laugh at his stories, shouted over the endless grumblings of the surf. To know that some part of whatever warmth was alive in his heart was because of me. Over a year since I last made the trip—sat by his throbbing sucking stove, drank strong black tea, lost at chess, fixed the front step.

Never again. Shit.

Autumn clings to branches. My mantra all the winding way—shitshitshitshitshit…

They've got what's left of Homer in a zippered bag. Corporal Desh and another cop load the bag into the cedar box in the back of my truck. Olivia Astrakhan told me they'd never in a million years let me transport the body to the crematorium myself—but I ask nicely and they do. I sign all the papers without reading them.

I appreciate all you've done, I say. It must have been pretty awful.

Part of the job, says Desh. He shrugs. Funny little place he had out there. Lonely as hell, I guess.

My father was an introvert, I say.

Maybe. Went a little squirrelly in the end—wouldn't you say?

I take Homer for a drive. The clouds are breaking open in the west and on an impulse I turn toward the light, aware of the cargo in the box of my truck like a crate of eggs. I feel every bump, but I open it up—accelerate into the turns—faster every time, driving the road west the way Homer used to drive it. With me—holding on to my seat belt—pressing my feet to the floor of his old white Toyota—praying we don't meet a logging truck or take a deer through the windshield.

I am alive. I can feel the heat in my blood, the electricity in my nerves, the patient labouring marrow in my bones. Very much alive. Sun clangs through a wrinkle in the unfolding clouds. I think for a while that I must be taking Homer back to Bone Island. (Or is *he* really taking *me?*) Away from lawyers and wills and funerals—away from my mother and my sister and Katherine—away from the questions, the suspicions, the accusations—away—west into the opening light, seeking the simplicity of rock and sky and sea. But I stop when I get to the ocean. I leave Homer in the truck and walk up the beach.

A small child, dwarfed by the universe, I sit on top of a giant drift-stump and wait for whales. It seems impossible that I must return to a world which imagines me a man in his forties—a good tradesman, a fair boss, father of a tall brilliant son.

Homer never grew up. Why must I?

When I was fourteen my father grew a beard and bought a motorcycle. We were Americans, then—all except my mother, who came from Montréal. (It's funny, because we are all Canadians, now, *except* my mother.) We lived in a white house with green shutters in the Berkshire Hills of Massachusetts, not far from the New York state line.

My mother taught in a private school. Homer was working on his third novel. (Or was it his fourth?) He'd almost sold the second one to a New York publisher, but they had asked him to change the ending and—of course—he refused.

One summer, Homer took me on the back of his motorcycle across the state line to watch a bunch of bands play rock and roll in a field. It rained like all the gods pissing at once. My sister was mad we didn't take her.

I remember every twist and turn of those country roads, my skinny arms wrapped around Homer's leather-jacketed waist, eating bugs and holding on for much more than dear life. I think I owned my own mortality in those moments as I seldom have since, but I was not afraid to die, only to let go—to lose the warm breathing solidity of my father—to let that strange rare closeness slip away. As if I knew—holding him tight—that nothing could hurt me really, nothing, not even shattered bone slashing through flesh, not even death, if I could only hold on to him.

The wind comes up off the strait but I sit like a statue on a stump, wondering when the predictable stages of grief are going to kick in, fill this horrible void left where alive Homer isn't. When the breeze picks up the sea and flings a handful in my face, I get back in my truck and drive toward home. Homer and I don't exchange a word.

The rain has been and gone, leaving puddles on Speed Avenue. Bonnie is in the kitchen making applesauce, wonderful bubbling cinnamon smells. Adam called, she says. Sylvie called and told him. I thought *you* were going to call him.

I meant to, I say.

He thinks we should have the memorial thingy next weekend. He can't get over till then, anyway. He's got midterms all week.

27

Isn't next weekend Hallowe'en?

Yeah. Kind of appropriate for a funeral, maybe?

Do we come in costume?

That's what Adam said—he must be your kid after all. I told him I didn't think that was exactly good taste.

I don't know, I say. Where's the good taste in drinking yourself into a naked stupor on the beach and letting the crows eat you?

Hey, he's *your* father. Don't ask me how I ever got involved with a bunch like *you*. Sure, let's come in costume. Maybe we should cancel the cremation—hang Homer's bones up on the porch with a glass of whiskey in his hand and a candle in his rib cage. Scare the living bejesus out of the trick-or-treaters.

I should call my mother, I say.

Hey, did you see this? Bonnie shoves the paper at me:

Local Writer Dead

Local author and book-seller Homer Knee was found dead earlier this week near his Bone Island home. Knee, the author of a number of underground classic novels, was, for many years, the popular proprietor of Esoterica Used Books.

I chuckle. Bonnie snorts. Underground classic novels? she says. Shouldn't she mention that the reason they were so underground was that he never managed to convince anybody to publish them?

At least she got in a plug for the store, I say.

Midweek—late night—moon breaking through. Bonnie just called on her midnight break to say goodnight. Brushing my teeth when the phone rings.

Hello?

Mr. Knee?

Speaking.

Is this a secure line? Can we be sure we are alone?

I'm alone. Who is this?

A friend of your father's. I don't want to say more over the phone. Can we meet?

A friend of Homer's? What's your name?

You don't know it. Homer never told anyone about me. And I never told anyone about him. It was part of our agreement. Are you alone there?

Here? Yes.

I'll be there in five minutes. The back door. I won't knock—be there to let me in. Five minutes.

Hey, wait a minute—

Relax, Larry. It's seventeen minutes past the hour. Five minutes.

The voice in the phone seemed to come from a substantial person, a person of stature—a paranoid, certainly, but probably a paranoid with connections. The ghost who slips by me and up the back stairs—at exactly twenty-two minutes past—seems like nobody, in comparison. Small, slight, vaguely androgynous, his face charged with a kind of boyish arrogant innocence—a youthful look belied by the close-cropped hair, shot through with grey. He might be a prematurely grey twenty-five year old, or a smooth-faced fifty.

He wears a black baseball cap with the brim to the back—no monogram—a black sweat suit, black runners. He looks like a cat burglar, and he moves like one, smooth, quick and silent, room to room, making sure we really are alone. He moves confidently through my little house, giving me the creeps.

I fill the kettle. A million thoughts. Well—two or three, anyway. I never in a million years thought my father might be gay—but who the hell *is* this guy, then? And what is the nature of his *agreement* with Homer? Or is he a spy (sent by Katherine?) nosing around looking for the missing book? Maybe he really *is* just a cat burglar. Any moment, frustrated to find no TV or VCR, he may turn ugly.

Finally he deems it safe to offer me his hand and a name. Arthur Humble, he says. Call me Art. It's an honour to finally meet you.

Why?

I've got a lot of respect for the life you've chosen—even if it wasn't always what your father might have wished for you. And *he* had a lot of respect for you too, you know.

No, I say. I wasn't asking why you are honoured to meet me.

That stops him for a second. Oh—he says. You mean the security concern—jumping the back fence, all that? Sorry. Probably unnecessary, but there is always time to take precautions, don't you think? It will be better if I can remain in the background—out of the picture, as it were.

As *what* were? Who *are* you, *Art*? Does this have something to do with the missing manuscript?

So it's true, then—you don't have it?

I really don't. Do you?

Hey, I'm not much on the kind of stuff your father wrote. Over my head a little, if you know what I mean. I go for a good whodunit, myself. That's how I came to know your father, you know. He used to put the good ones aside for me. I always told him he should write one himself.

You were a customer?

Why don't we get right to the point, Mr. Knee?

Please. What's the point?

I want to know who murdered your father. Don't you?

Bonnie finds me in the kitchen, staring at two full mugs of stone cold tea.

Jesus, she says. You haven't been entertaining ghosts again, have you?

I'm not sure, I say. I try to tell her about Art Humble.

He calls himself a private investigator. Emphasis on the private. He claims Homer was his client for years, though on what business exactly he won't say. He claims Homer had enemies, but he won't say who or why. He implies that everything at the bookstore wasn't always on the up and up—that some other form of merchandise might have been passing through Homer's hands. Drugs? Kiddy porn? Art's not saying. He's suspicious of Katherine, but then he's suspicious of Olivia Astrakhan, too, and of Liz.

Your mother?

I know. He kind of lost *me* there, too. He claims she's never let go of Homer. Maybe he's right. Isn't she flying all the way out here from New York this weekend just to drink a toast to his ashes?

Hey, says Bonnie. I wouldn't put *anything* past *your* family.

He was pissed off we'd had Homer cremated. I told him the autopsy found no signs of foul play, but he said that by the time the vultures got through—it would have been hard to tell much.

He seriously thinks somebody killed Homer for his book?

I don't know. There's something else. Some whole secret chapter of Homer's life he won't even *refer* to—except in this really veiled way. You can feel it crowding him, though, all the time…

Hey, says Bonnie. We only found out Homer was dead what—less than a week ago? Already we've turned up a lawyer and a private eye we didn't know existed. Maybe there's a *few* chapters of Homer's life we haven't scratched yet. Where did Homer hook up with this character, anyway?

At the book store, I guess. Art was some nerdy adolescent who came around looking for detective stories and Homer took an interest. Steered him away from the pulp a little—got him reading Chandler and Conan Doyle and Poe. Young Art wanted to detect, so Homer gave him his first job.

What sort of job?

Investigating. Art's not saying any more.

I know it sounds crazy, Larry—but what if he's right? What makes him think Homer was murdered, anyway?

He insists that Homer wouldn't have undertaken anything as serious as suicide without informing him. I don't believe any of it, Bonnie. Is Homer really dead? Are those really his ashes over there on top of the fridge? Art Humble seems too unlikely to exist. Maybe I dreamt him—like I dreamt Homer's ghost that time.

Or maybe Homer's ghost really did come. Maybe he was trying to tell you something. Like the ghost in Hamlet.

I don't know, Bonnie—I don't think it's Shakespeare. It feels more like the plot of one of Homer's worst novels.

So what does this Art guy really want?

He wants me to hire him to find out who killed Homer—
and to track down the missing manuscript. He implied that if I
were to employ him he might not keep his cards nailed quite so
firmly to his chest. As it were.

You think he cooked up the whole paranoid scenario just to
try to hook you?

Seems as likely as anything else.

I take it you didn't bite?

I told him I'd think about it.

Bonnie laughs. He's not much of a detective if he hasn't figured out you are too cheap to pay somebody to do your worrying
for you, she says.

Later, when Bonnie is asleep, I wonder why I didn't tell her the one
bit of gossip Art Humble did tell me about Katherine. *You know—
she was just a street punk when your father took her in*, he said.

She was young, I said.

Art snorted. *She came into your father's bookstore with a replica handgun—tried to rob him.*

*You're joking. What a peculiar thing to do. Did she steal some
of his first editions?*

*She was a heroin addict. She'd heard rumours on the street that
the bookstore was just a front for something more lucrative.*

Was it?

*I'm not here to tell tales on the dead. But when that girl waved
a gun in his face your father laughed at her. He showed her the contents of his cash-box—offered it to her in exchange for the gun. In
case he had to fend off any more robbers, he said. She confessed that
the gun was a fake. All the better, he said, he didn't want to hurt anybody. They had a cup of tea to seal the deal, as it were.*

D inner at Leila and Duncan's, the night before Homer's memorial. My mother wears a red dress and drinks vodka. Duncan does lasagna—offers me a beer. Leila wears a grey suit, drinks red wine. Adam and Sylvie disappear into the basement, ostensibly to try out Duncan's new pool table.

Bonnie wouldn't come. Tell them I'm sick, she said. Tell them I'm coming down with the same thing that killed Homer. I'll see them all tomorrow at the thing.

My mother is disappointed. You don't think I came all this way to see you, she says to me.

I thought you came to see Homer. Off.

Oh yes, that, she says. Did the bugger have the sense to leave a will at least?

Apparently. I called Olivia Astrakhan. She's coming tomorrow. She suggested we could get together after and run though it.

I wonder if poor Homer ever got into her pants. He had a bone for her so bad when our divorce was going through—I almost felt sorry for him. Is she still gorgeous?

Jesus Christ, Mother, says Leila.

I only spoke to her on the phone, I say. How's Walter?

Walter's Walter. Only these days he's Saint Walter.

My mother seems the same as she has always been—which makes it seem all the more unlikely that my father should be so dead. Duncan opens me another beer.

So—poor Homer is to suffer his final humiliation in a cos-

34

metics warehouse under construction? my mother says. This was *your* idea, Larry?

Bonnie's actually. Only I think she was joking.

Well, why not? Homer wouldn't have been caught dead in a church, or anything resembling one. He certainly left *that* all far behind—once he'd buried *his* mother. Now *there* was a terrifying woman. She had a hot wire up her butt and a glare that could peel fruit. I remember *her* funeral—it was the last time I ever saw Homer in a suit. He was drunk, of course, but I don't think anybody could tell but me. They all thought it was grief.

We talked about having the memorial at the bookstore, I say, but there just isn't room. Too full of books.

Don't mind me, Larry—Bonnie is perfectly right. This warehouse project is the first thing you and Leila have cooperated on in a very long time and I think Homer would feel honoured to be memorialized in the midst of your joint work-in-progress. We'll buy lots of flowers and pretty the place up.

Actually, says Leila, the warehouse is Duncan's baby. I haven't had much to do with it.

Never downplay the value of capital, dear—especially when *you* are the one supplying it. Liz hands Duncan her empty glass. Duncan puts a lot of vodka and a little ice in it and hands it back. I can tell he doesn't much like where this is going.

Larry and the gang are doing a fine job, he says.

I thought Leila was joking when she told me you were buying property on the corner of Alpha and Omega.

I thought she was joking when she asked me to look at the plans and give her a bid on it, I say.

Duncan's lasagna is surprisingly tasty. He's made two—one vegetarian for Adam and Sylvie. I try both. The vegetarian is better.

35

Duncan is taking a cooking course over the internet, says Leila. My mother almost chokes on her salad. Adam and Sylvie help themselves to seconds. When I first knew him, says Leila, he couldn't boil water without calling his mother.

Well, says Liz, cleaning her pipes with a big swallow of vodka, it's a good thing *one* of you is learning to cook. You could fit most of Walter's apartment into that kitchen of yours—it would be a shame not to use it.

More salad, Mother?

Don't mind me, dear. I always despised cooking myself, as you know, but in those days, of course, one had no choice. Thank God I found Walter. Walter's risotto gives me orgasms. Homer wasn't a bad cook, actually, when he wasn't half-cut. He used to make lovely jellies and preserves. He loved picking the fruit— standing over the kettle of steaming frothing syrup.

Singing, I say.

That's right. He had a beautiful baritone voice when he was younger. He could have sung opera with a little training. I used to tell him that. But of course he preferred sea shanties and drinking songs. Will there be music at the funeral?

Sylvie has offered to bring her fiddle, I say.

Lovely. I don't suppose you know *MacPherson's Lament*, my dear? That was one of Homer's favourites.

That's what Larry told me—I found it on a record at the library. I've been practicing it.

Wonderful. We won't ask you to smash your fiddle, of course. It's funny thinking about Homer's voice—it must be ten years since we spoke, but I can hear his voice like he's here in the room—feel the timbre of it, filling me up with words rich as chocolate. You know, before she died I got to know Homer's mother a little. She told me once that when Homer was a child he suffered from a speech impediment. The finer sounds—the r and l and some of the diphthongs—got tangled on his tongue and came out blunted, rounded off. She told me it persisted into his early teens. Homer never spoke of it himself—and I never brought it up—never let him know that his mother had told me. But I've wondered sometimes if the shame of it didn't have something to do with turning him into the misanthrope he became.

What exactly *is* a misanthrope? Sylvie wants to know.

Somebody who hates everybody, says Adam.

Did he really? says Sylvie. I mean—I know he moved off way off on that island all by himself and everything, but—I don't know—he just seemed so *kind*...

Leila laughs, so coldly that we all look at her. Liz looks the hardest, then shakes her head, pushes her plate away, pulls her glass close. No, dear, she says to Sylvie. He didn't hate *everybody*. And you are absolutely right—he *was* kind. He was a big man with a large warm heart, but he was never comfortable in his own skin. He was painfully shy. When we met he was nearly thirty and still a virgin. And not for want of libido—that's for sure. Once I got him started he didn't want to stop. But that's another story.

He's stopped now, points out Leila.

Bonnie is already in bed when Adam and I get home, after dropping Sylvie off at her mother's. Adam and I say goodnight on the stairs.

Liz sure seemed to be drinking a lot tonight, says Adam.

It's Homer's influence, I think.

She never got over him, did she?

She hated his guts but she loved his mind. No, I guess she never did get over him.

Sleep well, Larry, he says, hugging me.

Bonnie moves over, lets me have her warm spot. I lie there and wonder about tomorrow. The whole thing seems so ad hoc all of a sudden—so improvised—this dysfunctional family gathering around the ashes of a kind-hearted misanthrope in a half-built warehouse where Alpha Street intersects Omega Place—on the evening of the night when the dead are said to walk abroad. Just a tad disrespectful, maybe?

My mother will buy flowers. Sylvie will play her fiddle and we'll say our good-byes. What to say? Good-bye, Dad? Sorry I never really stopped to get to know you. It never occurred to me you'd actually go and die. Here lies Homer—uncomfortable in his skin, his family, his life—full of contradiction and shame and bitter disappointment. But he used to carry me on his shoulders and he loved me—I know he did. Don't I?

I wonder if I should get up and poke through the cardboard box under my desk—the one labeled **HOMER**—where I've kept copies of some of his early manuscripts, and tucked away the few letters he's written since moving out to Bone Island. Maybe I'd find something in there I could read at the ceremony. Something appropriate. But weariness sits on me like a draught horse and I don't get up…

I dream we are preparing the warehouse for Homer's memorial, but the walls of *this* warehouse are built not of bricks but of books—piles and piles of books, right up to the roof—the stacks sway a little as I move past them. Homer is there in the cedar coffin I built, and he is perfect, whole, composed, as if he only sleeps, or perhaps has only just passed on, quietly, in the middle of an amusing dream. The mourners begin to gather in full masquerade. Witches and devils and ghosts and goblins swirl past in a wild funeral dance. Only Bonnie and I are not in costume. We are both naked and Bonnie is carrying a new-born baby—and I have a red ribbon tied around my erection.

Hallowe'en day is dark and the wind is steady, damp and cold. Liz buys about a thousand dollars worth of flowers, which make Duncan's unfinished warehouse seem less like a construction site and more like a construction site full of flowers. Bonnie and I put a sheet of plywood on two saw horses, spread one of Bonnie's old lace tablecloths over it, set Homer in the middle, in his urn—flanked by black candles. Liz and Leila and Adam and Sylvie distribute and arrange the flowers. Duncan pretends he is too busy working to help, but manages to get in the way.

Well, says my mother—checking her watch—we've done what we can. I'll take everybody out to lunch. Everybody turns out to be me and Bonnie and Leila. Adam and Sylvie have to catch a bus—they are meeting some of Adam's friends up at the university. Duncan excuses himself—he's on a diet, has some paperwork to catch up on.

We run into Katherine at the door. Homer hated cut flowers, she says.

You must be Katherine, says my mother. I'm so happy to finally meet you, dear. I'm Liz. You are quite right, dear—Homer had no taste at all.

I just came by to see if I could help out. Looks like I'm not needed.

We were just heading out for a bite of lunch, dear. My treat. Why don't you join us?

Katherine starts to reply in the instinctive negative, but as she avoids my mother's penetrating gaze her eyes light on the urn which contains all that is left of Homer.

I'm not hungry, she says, but you can buy me a coffee.

Lunch at The Pit Road Café. Bonnie and I share a club sandwich. My mother has Swiss steak and spikes her coffee from a silver flask which she pulls out of her purse. Leila winces, trying to make herself invisible. My mother catches Katherine's eye. Katherine pushes her cup over.

The black candles were a nice touch, says Mother.

I picked them up a few weeks ago, on sale, says Bonnie. I thought they'd be good for Hallowe'en.

Here's to Homer, says Katherine, lifting her cup.

Here's to Hallowe'en, suggests my mother.

We drink coffee, eat fries and watch the wind lash the wires over the parking lot, listen to the hissing of the traffic up on Burnside. My mother asks Katherine about the business.

I imagine Homer left you with a bit of a mess when you took over? she says.

Homer had a unique approach to record keeping, admits Katherine.

Well put, my dear. I understand you've made quite a success of things, though?

We're getting by.

Homer was very lucky to find you, my dear. I hope you know how much we all appreciate everything you did for him.

Maybe, says Katherine, it would have been nice if you had let Homer know that.

Touché, dear. You're absolutely right. But don't deny an old woman a few petty jealousies to liven up her dotage. Too bad he went and died on you.

He'd written a book, says Katherine. A novel.

So I understand. I was going to ask you—was it any good? I always thought a little sobriety might go a long way to help him focus on whatever it was he was always so all-fired anxious to say.

He felt it was very good, says Katherine. *He* felt it was the

40

only thing he'd ever written that was worth *anything*. The last time I saw him he told me he was almost finished. *It's not easy to eat shit*, he said, *and I've eaten a truckload to write this*. He was holding the manuscript on his knees when he said that—like a baby or a pizza box or something. He never left me alone with it.

He was always very secretive about his work, says my mother.

I think I could have sold a collection of short stories for him, says Katherine, but he wouldn't let me. I'd placed a few of them in little magazines, you know—stories he wrote years ago and forgot—stuff I found when I cleaned out the back of the shop. He only let me send the stories out when I agreed to submit them under a pen-name, and he wouldn't let me market a collection. He said he didn't want to dilute the impact of the novel. He was so confident that he had finally done it—that this was *it*—his one shot. He didn't want to screw it up.

Dear God, says my mother. Listen to that wind. I think we'd better have another little taste. Larry? She produces the silver flask. I push my cup across—Bonnie covers hers with her hand. Leila excuses herself, goes to the washroom. Mother pours Katherine's last, saying, And what about you then, dear? What do *you* write?

Katherine shrugs. Before I took over the shop full-time I was working on a novel, she says. I haven't even *looked* at it in months.

Here's to real life, suggests my mother, lifting her cup.

I drink the whiskey-fragrant cream-heavy coffee and hear the wind cracking branches two blocks over on Speed Avenue, and I envision Homer at his Bone Island desk, with the withering gaze of the winter sea staring hard across his window. I picture him spooning up page after page of his own purple prose, shovelling it down.

I'm suddenly glad I never got it together to get up last night—to rummage in the cardboard box (labeled **HOMER** in

41

black felt pen) near the back of the cardboard box filing system under my slab door desk at home. It will be better just to speak from my heart. If I have one.

Home to change—I *do* look *at* the box under my desk. I can just see the corner of it peeking out between the box labeled **LARRY/PERSONAL** and the one labeled **MISC**. In spite of my resolution, I actually bend over to extricate it—but at that moment Adam raps on the window. He and Sylvie—on the porch—breathless, foot-wiping. Adam has something wrapped up in his blue handkerchief. He handles it gently, like something alive. We gather as he unfolds it on the kitchen counter. A tangle of small brown long-stemmed mushrooms.

Holy shit, says Bonnie. Where'd you find those?

Up at the university. They grow on the chip trails.

Adam selects a couple of the small flesh-like caps, rinses them under the tap, chews them slowly.

Feeling like I'm riding on the back of a motorcycle on a mountain road—holding on with all my life to the back of a mad-man—riding four cups of strong Pit Road coffee and a few splashes of my mother's American whiskey—I reach out and select the largest mushroom—pop it, unwashed, into my mouth. It tastes like dirt. I feel a tightening at the back of my throat.

Bonnie shakes her head. On top of a club sandwich? she says.

By the time we get back to the warehouse the wind has dropped; the air is so still you can almost see it. I outgrew my last dark suit twenty-five years ago; I wear my best jeans and my brightest yellow sweater. Bonnie wears her red dress—the same one she wore when she finally agreed to marry me. Adam wears black, as always. Sylvie comes in real sackcloth, and barefoot. She's got her fiddle.

A corner of one of the tarps has blown loose from the loading dock door. My mother and Leila and Duncan all stand, necks craned, staring up into the darkness where a young sea gull shrieks and shuffles restlessly along the bottom chord of one of the trusses.

Olivia Astrakhan is still beautiful. Black suit, black briefcase, silver pendant moon, blue eye-liner. She smells like a vanilla cookie. She shakes my hand warmly and smiles and takes in the whole scene—from the screaming bird in the trusses to the pallets of block and piles of lumber at the far end of the building— from Homer in his urn on his sawhorse table, among guttering black candles stuck in empty Black Tower wine bottles, to Sylvie in sackcloth playing beautiful dirges into the merciless acoustics of the pressure drop. When she meets my eyes again she is still smiling. I notice, for the second time, how beautiful she is. I also notice—for the first time—how much she looks like a mushroom.

Katherine comes in jeans and a baggy maroon sweater. Kate

wears black leather.

Hey, Larry, says Kate. Cool place for a funeral, man. How you doing?

Okay.

Man, it's eerie out there. So quiet after that wind, and dark. I think we're going to get it. What the hell was that?

A sea gull. One of the tarps blew open while we were gone for lunch. I guess he flew in to get out of the storm.

Katherine goes white.

A few strangers. Most of them seem to know Katherine—old customers from the bookstore, I guess. A couple introduce themselves—Greta, from Oak Bay, who describes herself as a collector—Liam, a double amputee, who describes himself as a man of the streets. A buxom redhead in a sleek black dress shakes my hand warmly. She seems extremely familiar, but it is not until she speaks—introducing herself as Artemis Hamilton, please call me Art—that I recognize Art Humble in drag.

Sylvie rosins her bow, gives us a little Mozart, melting at length into *MacPherson's Lament*. She dances alone with her fiddle, barefoot in the far dark. She's very good, says my mother. Suzuki method, I suppose? Is Katherine going to be all right? She doesn't look well.

She wasn't ready for the uninvited guest, I say, pointing at the bird in the trusses. She had to fight them for his bones, I guess.

Dear me. Perhaps this wasn't such a good idea. I'm beginning to think you may be right, Larry. Maybe she hasn't got the book. I'm beginning to wonder if she has the moral courage for *anything*.

Bonnie wants me to dance. In my family we always dance at funerals, she says. Bonnie has a large close family, always ready to support her—to welcome her back, to celebrate with her—

44

although they exist only in her imagination.

Leila wants me to be in charge. I can see right through her—she is naked inside her clothes. I've never noticed how much she looks like a mushroom.

I dance with my Bonnie Secret.

Who's the floozy with the big bazoombas? Bonnie wants to know as I whirl her away from the halogen lamps, into the dusty shadows.

Art Humble, I tell her.

She steps on both my feet.

My mother takes charge.

I don't think anyone else is coming, she announces, so we may as well get on with it. I'm going to speak first, since I've known Homer the longest, and come the farthest to be here. First, I'd like to apologize for the lack of chairs. We were going to rent chairs, but somebody pointed out that it was too cold in here to sit around, and we were too cheap to rent heaters as well—so there you are.

I'd forgotten how good my mother could look—with a crowd, a classroom, a lecture hall, in the palm of her hand. But Bonnie interrupts her. If we are going to stand, she says, I think we should make a circle around Homer's ashes and join hands.

My mother is nonplussed—but Adam takes her right hand and Sylvie her left and suddenly we are a circle. The last to join is Katherine. Kate already has one of her hands, and after a few moments hesitation she gives the other to Liam in his wheelchair, completing the circle. Homer hated this kind of thing, she says.

Of course he did, says my mother. He was terrified of circles. In his heart he always wanted to be in the center. Now he is.

For a time we stand and feel the sudden surprising energy

45

captured in our simple act of union. When Mother speaks again, her mood has changed perceptibly. I am not used to speaking without the use of my hands, she says. Perhaps I depend too much on sleight-of-hand where the naked truth should do…

I met Homer at a funeral—my brother's. They were friends at college. Alex died in a climbing accident. He was a fool—a show-off—my favourite brother of course. The war was barely over and nothing was more unnecessary than his death, though it did bring Homer into my life. I was engaged to another man, but I'd never met anybody who had what Homer had. I'd never real-ized what fakes and impostors we all were till I met Homer. He was so very *real*. Of course I realized later that was *his* front. He looked good in a black suit, by the way. He was skinny as a rail in those days, which made him look even taller. He still limped a lit-tle, from his war wound, though that hadn't stopped him making it up the rock face which moments later would kill my brother…

My mother was taken with him. At least he was not a Jew, like the communist I was engaged to marry when I met him. My mother invited him to stay the weekend with us. I was supposed to meet my fiancé at some political rally. I cancelled.

Homer was the smartest person I'd ever met. In those days I was dumb enough to still find sheer brilliance extremely attrac-tive. He knew stuff about stuff I didn't even know was stuff, and I'd graduated Phi Beta Kappa and Magna Cum Laude and all that Greek and Latin racket. Homer could think rings around me. I sort of liked it for a while, but eventually it made me dizzy and gave me a headache and after a while he didn't bother any more. He could have done anything—I'm convinced of it—if he hadn't chosen to think rings around himself, instead, and then have a few drinks to unwind…

I won't pass judgement on him as a father—his children are here—they can do that if they feel the need. As a husband he sucked rocks, frankly. Please pardon my tongue—I live in New York. And I mean no disrespect to the dead. Homer never aspired to husbandhood—he had other things on his mind. His beautiful terrible mind. I didn't come all this way to argue with you, Homer. What is at stake here? The chance of personal happiness? I hope you found some, Homer. You died as ugly as you lived, wrestling your own evil angel. Katherine is right—you would have hated this. You preferred the intense fetid flowers of the bogs and swamps. But you left us bright moments and there was great good in your heart. I had a whole lot more to say but I won't ramble on. I only came to say good-bye…Good-bye, Homer.

Again we stand, and even the bird in the trusses is silent. The barometric pressure drops another kilo-Pascal. Katherine clears her throat.

I knew the real Homer, she says. He cared nothing for any of this. He was passionately devoted to his work; it meant *everything* to him. The scorn and rejection heaped on his head only strengthened his belief in the value of his own vision. This kind of story is supposed to have a happy ending. Perseverance furthers. He who laughs last, laughs best. Homer isn't laughing, and neither am I. If anybody in this room—in this circle—knows what's become of his final manuscript, I only hope that they will someday grant the rest of us a chance to see it—to read it and judge for ourselves.

People are looking at me. I want to protest my innocence, but I can't help feeling maybe they all know something I don't. I've never noticed how much we *all* look like mushrooms—a fairy ring! Adam speaks. He stands directly across the circle from me, between Liz and Bonnie. I see him framed in flowers as he speaks to his grandfather.

Thank you, Grandpa Homer, he says. Thank you for everything. Thank you for teaching me the names of the stars and what they are like, but also what they mean. Thank you for teaching me chess and other games, and for teaching me that the *game* is nothing—the *move* is everything. Thank you for teaching me to love books, for their smell and feel, and weight and power.

Thank you, Grandpa Homer, for never being ordinary—even living in times when maybe it was more than expected of you. And thank you for being so wise without making me feel stupid.

Again silence. And then the wind, shaking angry applause out of the tarps. I look at Leila. Everyone else is looking at me. I guess I should say something—but Sylvie clears her throat.

I hardly really knew Homer, she says, though I am very fond of his grandson. I remember, once, when I was small, my mother took me into his book store. I don't know why—she never read books. I think maybe we ducked in to get out of the rain—I don't remember. But I do remember the wonderful smell of all those old books. And Homer. Even then he seemed old to me—with his big grey beard. He was singing to himself, on top of his ladder—shelving books and singing. It was a song I'd never heard, but I thought it was very beautiful and very sad. I've remembered it ever since. There are verses to the song—I heard them later but I only remember Homer singing the chorus.

And she sings—her beautiful soprano voice hanging in the echoing space, long after it leaves her throat—

> *Fare thee well for I must leave thee,*
> *Do not let this parting grieve thee,*

For remember that the best of friends must part.
Adieu, adieu, kind friends, adieu.
I can no longer stay with you.
I'll hang my heart in the weeping willow tree—
and may the world go well with thee.

I remember standing like this once, I say, when the echoes finally ebb away. I was almost still just a kid—standing like this—holding my father's big warm hand, on the other side of me a woman I did not know, her hands cool and smooth and no bigger than my own, our circle joined—a chain we just had to believe was big enough and strong enough to encircle the evil that stared us in the face—the five-sided fortress—the troops with bayonets fixed—the low rolling cloud of choking gas. The Pentagon didn't rise. Well—not enough, anyway. The circle was broken. Shortly after we fled the country—

A sudden gust of wind snaps one of the tarps with a report loud as a gunshot. The gull lets loose a blood-curdling shriek and flaps down from the trusses, landing with a clunk beside Homer's urn on the table. One of the candles falls to the floor and gutters out. Katherine yelps like a stepped-on pup. The bird stands there for a moment—giving us all the eye—then leaps flapping into the air, sending three more candles and the urn itself rolling onto the concrete slab. The gull makes several wild shrieking circuits of the space—sending the strings of temporary lights dancing and making the shadows swim. Finally it settles among the trusses again, composes itself and shits all over Olivia Astrakhan's black briefcase.

Katherine is in Kate's arms. The circle is broken. Adam recovers the urn—Bonnie sets right the candles. Duncan gets a box of tissues from his office for Olivia. Bonnie gives me a nudge and I raise my hand in the air and stand there until they are all

49

looking at me again. Pizza and hot chocolate at our place, I say. Everybody's welcome.

Pizza boxes burn brightly in the fireplace. Katherine is stretched out on the sofa, her head in Kate's lap. Leila and Duncan closeted in the music room—yelling at each other as quietly as they can. Sylvie and Adam carve a jack-o'-lantern with my mother in the kitchen. I make chocolate chip cookies for the trick-or-treaters. Some of them look at me askance but they all take the cookies. No faint-hearted spooks venture down Speed Avenue. Bonnie has gone to lie down. Art Humbleton sits in the corner, pretending to drink a diet Coke. Olivia opens her briefcase.

Maybe we should get this over with, Larry.

Homer leaves Katherine his share of the book store. She doesn't smile. My mother smiles, says—Well, my dear, I guess we are officially partners, at last. You have my absolute trust in everything, of course.

We all stare at her till she frowns and says, Well, where did you *think* he got the money to buy a book store?

He leaves my sister Leila his savings, which Olivia estimates—roughly—at an after-tax amount astounding to all of us. My mother frowns; Katherine glares at her. Leila looks perplexed, almost offended. Duncan grins.

Homer leaves me Bone Island—and all the rights to his literary estate.

What will you do with the ashes? asks Olivia, as I help her on with her coat.

I thought we should scatter them at Bone Island. It's the place he loved best.

You realize, of course, that he never had legal title. That legacy is meaningless, in legal terms. I told him that, but he insisted I put it in.

It's the thought that counts, I say.

A shame about the book, she says. But maybe he knew best.

Art is in the kitchen, playing cards with Adam and Sylvie. My mother has emptied her silver flask (again) and gone to lie down. I say goodbye to Katherine and Kate on the porch; Kate kisses me and Katherine says, I'll call you. I'd still like to put together that book of his short stories. It's up to you now, of course.

Call me, I say.

It is raining, steady, straight down, not a breath of wind. Worms drown.

Watch out for that Hamilton woman, says Katherine, turning, halfway down the steps.

You're not serious, I say.

She was just a punk kid when Homer took pity on her, says Katherine. She tried to rob the book store with a toy gun. Thought Homer was some kind of big time racketeer—that the book store was a front for something. Homer took the gun away—gave her a cup of tea—sent her home with a stack of hard-covers.

You're joking.

That's the story Homer told me.

Two steps more and she turns again.

I had an idea for a title for that book of stories. I thought of calling it *Everything but the Truth.* I'll call you.

Leila goes to wake my mother, who is passed out beside Bonnie in our bedroom. Duncan is still smiling. Nice piece of change, I say.

What's that, chief? Oh, yeah, a nice piece—who'd have imagined he'd have a bundle like that stashed away? I was figuring we'd all have to chip in just to cover expenses.

Life is weird. Listen, could you guys give Ms. Hamilton a lift? She lives out your way, I think.

Art flashes me a look but goes quietly. My mother—drunk and sleepy—kisses me wetly and apologizes. God, I'm sorry, Larry.

For what, Mother?

Leila has her arm—tries to move her toward the stairs. She's had too much to drink, Larry. We'll call you tomorrow.

I promised him you would never know. About the book store. It was our secret. I'm sorry, Larry—I should have kept my word. Take it from your poor old mother, Larry—don't make promises to dead people.

We'll call you, says Leila.

The cards are still all over the table, but Adam and Sylvie have disappeared downstairs. Bonnie is curled up on top of our bed—still in her wedding dress. I cover her with a blanket.

I put a couple of chunks of 2X4 on the coals and wait for flames. The urn with Homer's ashes sits on the mantel. The house full of the fragrance of the armfuls of cut flowers we hauled back with us from the warehouse. I get out my pipe. Rain drums on the porch roof, and somewhere down the street a brave soul sets off a screamer. Happy Hallowe'en.

And then I am aware of a different rhythm—a quiet squinch and giggle—trickling up from Adam's bedroom downstairs. I gaze out at the darkness. Most of the jack-o'-lanterns on Speed Avenue have drowned or guttered out. I half expect to see Homer—appropriately dressed for the weather this time—trudging up the steps.

He doesn't appear. Just two late trick-or-treaters—almost teenagers—dressed as devils. The cookies are gone so I give them the last of the pizza. Might as well tidy up a little. But when I stoop to retrieve a plate from under my desk, my eyes fall on that cardboard box again. I leave the plate, pull out the box instead.

I know—opening the cardboard box labeled **HOMER**— what I will find. The manuscript is right on top, wrapped in several plastic bags. Inside the penultimate plastic bag, I find a thick envelope with my name scrawled across it in Homer's unmistakably messy hand. The ultimate bag is sealed with enough duct tape to gag an elephant. I leave it and slit the envelope with my Swiss Army knife.

The letter is typed—the familiar erratic signature of Homer's venerable Olivetti:

Oct. 31

Dear Larry,

First, please forgive me the self-indulgence of post-dating this missive. A parlor trick, intended to impress, I admit it, and if I have missed the mark entirely then I really am dead and gone and lost forever.

Oh, Larry, my son, we who dare to try to communicate from beyond the grave walk a dangerous line, but--since the ultimate price is paid already--we may as well claim what ephemeral compensations remain.

I owe enough apologies to fill a book--hell, a library--and yet I am sorry for none of it; I regret nothing. I <u>do</u> owe a couple of explanations, which may or may not be contained within the few pages of this letter and/or the many pages of the manuscript enclosed. Please read this letter but--show it to no one.

<u>DO</u> <u>NOT</u> <u>READ</u> <u>THE</u> <u>MANUSCRIPT!</u>

I know I have hurt you, and I know also that I will hurt you more before I am through. Why then should I expect you to respect my wishes (demands?) from the other side of death? Am I wrong to trust you? Facing an end now so close and abrupt--looking back on a life that has given so little--am I wrong, in final desperation, to ask so much?

I need three things of you, Larry, my oldest son. First (and most important): <u>DO</u> <u>NOT</u> <u>READ</u> <u>THE</u> <u>BOOK!</u>

Second: Reveal to no one the contents of this letter!
Third: Deliver the manuscript into the hands of a certain person.

Of these three, I expect you will find the second
the most difficult of all--for I do include your dear
Bonnie in this prohibition. Please believe me that it is
for her sake--and yours--that I ask this of you. I cannot ask you to lie to her; I have always envied the
honesty I see between you. Therefore--in her case only
--I do not ask that you conceal the existence of this letter, but only the contents.

Yes, I called you my oldest son, and I know you
noticed that curious description. Even facing my own
mortality like a brick in the face--I cannot seem to be
direct. Yes, I have another son, and he is the person
to whom you will (I hope! I believe!) deliver the book.

I don't expect you to be shocked, or even surprised, although it may surprise you to learn that
your younger half-brother was conceived in a leaky
pup tent not far from the one where you slept through
most of that third and final night of music in Max
Yasger's back pasture--way back in the mythical summer of '69.

His mother (who still calls herself Zanzu) was
travelling with a man who would certainly have killed
us both if he had known, but he was dead drunk under
an alder bush at the time, and adventure was in the
air.

My younger son has never known of my existence.
He lives, convinced that the animal who slept that
night in his own vomit--the creature who has haunted
his mother's life ever since (when not in jail)--is really
his father.

As a living man, I always respected the wishes of
his mother. I let her exclude me from his life--although
I have availed myself of the services of a young inves-

tigator to keep myself informed of my son's where-
abouts and the course of his life.

Your half-brother's name is Y. This is not an ini-
tial but the full spelling. It is pronounced like the question. According to my most current information,
Zanzu--a tattoo artist--has a small studio near the village of Shawville, in the Pontiac region of western
Quebec. Her clients are mostly biker gangs and local
teens. Y lives somewhere in the hills nearby, and
makes his living as a bee-keeper.

I might have sent Y the manuscript, but I have
not dared to make a copy--lest it fall into the wrong
hands--and I have given too much of myself to this pile
of paper to trust the only copy in the hands of the
postal service. Besides, I flatter myself to think that
you and Y--my two sons--may find some common
ground, may touch through me (through this poor
manuscript of mine, at least) to become, somehow,
brothers at last. Therefore, I ask of you--my final
wish, Larry--that you put the thing into his hands with
your own, and explain to him that it is my first and
last and only legacy. His eyes will be--if you have not
betrayed me, Larry!--the first besides my own to scan
the contents of these pages. His heart, and his heart
alone, must decide the fate of this--my last creation. If
it displeases or offends him, then he may choose to
destroy it without trace. I pray that he will see in it
some good, and choose to share it, then, with you, and
perhaps later with the world. But the decision must be
his alone!

Don't trust A. H. (Who could?) Don't trust Katherine.
Both of them love me, but both are unreliable. Do
trust Olivia Astrakhan--up to a point. She will be
expecting to hear from you.

A sum of money has been set aside to cover the

expenses of your trip east. Olivia has received a copy
of this letter and will accompany you. There is every
possibility that the legacy you deliver will not be easily
welcomed, and I have no wish to send you into what
may become a sticky situation without <u>some</u> support.

In love and trust, your father, Homer Knee

p.s. You may wonder--since I ask you to trust Olivia--
why I have not left this matter in her hands. Two reasons. The first I have already stated above--my self-
indulgent hope that this delivery may lead eventually
to some sort of fraternal relationship between my two
stranger sons. The second I must stress here. I trust
Olivia--and you should trust her, too--but only up to a
point! <u>DO</u> <u>NOT</u> <u>LET</u> <u>HER</u> <u>HAVE</u> <u>ACCESS</u> <u>TO</u> <u>THE</u> <u>BOOK</u>!
She is possessed of enough curiosity to kill the cat
nine times and for good.

p.p.s. sorry I couldn't stay for tea

The fire is out. The noises from below have subsided back into the
background lust of the universe. I reread Homer's letter, fold it
up and put it back in the envelope. The blade of the Swiss Army
knife is still extended.

Maybe just a look. A roll of duct tape in the kitchen drawer—do it up again—no one need ever know.

I pick up the knife, put it down again. Realizing my hesitation has more to do with my own reluctance than any respect for
my dead father's wishes. After all the mystification, whatever real-
ity is trapped in this package can only be some sort of disappointment.

I pick up the knife again. I'm sitting there, using it to clean the dead skin from under my fingernails when Bonnie appears in the doorway, squinting and wrinkled in her red dress.

Oh, she says. You found it.

I put the knife down, look at her.

Sorry, she says. I found it day before yesterday. I thought I'd tell you tomorrow, once everything was over with. I thought that might be better.

You found it, I say, stupidly.

I'm not sure what made me look in there. I guess I'd been thinking about that dream you had—how vivid it was—how unlike a dream, you said. It just came to me that maybe it *wasn't* a dream—*or* a ghost. Maybe he really *did* come. Only why would he come, and then leave like that? It occurred to me that maybe he came to bring you the book. Only he didn't want you to find it right away—because he was afraid you might guess he was going to kill himself and try to stop him. So he put it where he knew you probably wouldn't look till after you heard he was dead. Once I got that far there weren't many places to look, really.

It sounds so obvious, when you put it like that. Did you read it?

Does it look like I read it?

I meant the letter.

It was sealed, wasn't it?

Sorry—of course. I'm a little freaked. You did the right thing, by the way. Not telling me. He wants me to keep it a secret. It would have been hard for me to get through today and not say anything.

Well, hey—after all his sneaking around, I didn't figure he wanted me to issue a press release.

Here, I say, handing her the letter.

Bonnie sits in my chair, smoothes the skirt of her dress, knits her brow.

It's dated today, she says.

A parlour trick, he says. Read it.

She does. A flicker of tolerant disdain crosses her countenance as she reads the opening paragraphs, quickly replaced by consternation.

What the fuck? she says. He doesn't want you to read the book?

Go on.

She does—frowning now—until she gets to the part about not telling her. She looks into my eyes. You aren't even supposed to be letting *me* read *this*, she says.

Maybe Homer misjudged me, I say. Maybe I'm *not* to be trusted.

I'd rather not believe that, Larry. She refolds the letter without reading any further, puts it back in the envelope.

Hell, Bonnie, I say, I don't know if I can be trusted or not, but I know *you* can trust me.

But can she? I dream of Olivia Astrakhan—her eyes dark and bright—her skin the colour of mushrooms.

Day dawns bright. The crystals hanging in our window break the light, streak the ceiling and blob the walls with bolts of spectral colour. Bonnie—wrapped up in the quilt—looks like a mummy with big hair. I know I am more in love with her at this moment than I have ever been, in twenty years, but I am not sure that is enough.

It is eight o'clock on a Sunday morning, but Olivia Astrakhan is in her office and answers on the second ring.

Hi, Larry.

You knew all along he'd left the book with me. Hidden it.

No, she says. I only found out last night. The only thing I didn't tell you was that he had left a sealed envelope—with instructions that I was to open it, alone in my office, after the reading of the will. I opened it last night, after I left you. Frankly—I'm a little freaked out, Larry. The letter is dated October thirty-first. Homer put that envelope in my hand over four months ago. It's been locked in my desk ever since. How did he do that, Larry?

I don't know. Not a fucking clue. A parlour trick.

He enclosed money, Larry—cash. Lots. For the trip, I guess. What am I missing, here, Larry? I mean—even if he knew *when* he was going to kill himself, and knew when Katherine would find him—and even if he could foresee that this weekend would be the first convenient date for a funeral—and even if he could guess, knowing his kin, that you would not resist the coincidence and would choose Hallowe'en for the ceremony—okay, maybe post-dating the letter is a good guess, a trick that came off. But how did he know you wouldn't find the book till last night? Did he know you *that* well? Or is there something else going on here?

I didn't think he knew me at all, I say. But maybe I was wrong.

I think you were wrong, she says. Can we get together and talk?

I'll be over in fifteen minutes.

The building is locked up. I'll have to come down and let you in.

She's wearing jeans and a blue-grey angora sweater. When she lets me in, she shakes my hand again, looks into my eyes and smiles. I wonder if *she's* been having dreams about *me*. I follow her up two flights of stairs, although there *is* an elevator. Maybe she's on a fitness kick—she's certainly in shape.

I wonder what Bonnie—at home in her mummy of covers—is dreaming about.

Olivia's office is small but bright, full of colourful posters of Greek Islands and Hawaiian volcanoes. A fig tree fills one corner with green. Windows on the street. She has a pot of coffee keeping warm, refills hers, pours a mug for me. It's decaf, I'm afraid, she says. I see you didn't bring the book with you. It's safe?

I put it back where I found it, I say. I guess it's safe—I just don't know from what. Bonnie actually found it first, a couple of days ago. She didn't tell me.

Did she read the letter?

Yes. No. Part of it. She didn't open it when she found it. I let her read it but when she got to the part about I wasn't supposed to tell her—she wouldn't read any more.

She respects Homer's wishes. That's nice. What about you, Larry? How well *did* he know you?

I haven't opened the package. It's—very well wrapped. I haven't peeked. But I'm not sure that has anything to do with Homer's wishes.

No?

No.

Surely you must be curious?

She meets my eyes again. Her irises are very dark, black walnut inlaid in ivory. Her own curiosity is palpable—almost sensual—and only some of it has to do with Homer's book. I remember what Homer said in the letter about her curiosity. I wonder if her copy of the letter included that p.s.?

I break away from her eyes, stand up, walk to the window. The antique shops across Fort Street are all closed; a man wearing a Santa hat walks a small pudgy dog. I was always pretty good at tests, I say. But I never liked them. That's one of the reasons I quit school.

I think maybe Homer knew you very well, she says. He certainly knew *me*. He knew I'd have broken down and ripped the thing open in an hour if he'd left it with me.

You kept his letter locked in a drawer for four months, I say.

Yes. That's true. But I thought he was alive. I'd never have dared betray him when he was alive.

You've known for a week that he was dead. Why did you wait till last night to open the letter?

I knew I'd have to face all of you—yesterday. I guess I was afraid I might—it might...I guess it seemed better to wait.

I knew I would have to face *you*—today.

I see what you mean. Some method in his madness?

Maybe.

Legally, of course, this letter means nothing, she says. The book remains part of his literary estate. As his literary executor you can do whatever you wish. There is no mention of this person Y in the will. Did you ever suspect something like this?

No. I mean—I knew *something* happened to Homer at Woodstock. I mean—I met her, you know, that girl—Zanzu. I remember her. I can see her in my mind—she had very very fine hair. They were camped right behind us. She would have been beautiful, except her teeth were yellow and crooked. She had this funny, kind of scary smile. She chain-smoked Camels—I can't picture her without one. I knew Homer had the hots for her, but I never—no.

I look out the window. I try to picture Homer—sleek, red-bearded, bellyless—making love with the willowy girl I dreamt of for months, maybe years, afterwards. I can almost see them, in my mind's eyes, through the rain, through the half open flap of the muddy pup tent. Homer has his leather jacket on. Zanzu lights a fresh cigarette off the butt of the last.

Olivia pulls out a drawer, takes out an envelope, extracts a thick stack of fifty-dollar bills, old ones—with the RCMP Musical Ride on the back, not the owl. She spreads them across the desk top like a winning hand.

Well, she says, if you want to go through with this, we can go first class.

What about you? I ask. You were his lawyer. Didn't you know anything about all this?

I knew Homer had secrets. He was a very creative bookkeeper. I sometimes suspected that some of the rumours about his business were not necessarily untrue. I even knew that he occasionally employed a cross-dressing paranoid who claimed to be a private investigator—but who has never been *licensed* as such in any jurisdiction *I'm* aware of. Homer paid this person cash. Homer liked cash. But I never did find out exactly what Homer paid this person to do.

Her hands move slowly over the spread notes, as if she is warming them over a slow fire. I get the feeling *she* likes cash, too. Her nails are perfect.

Surely you must have been curious? I say. She catches the echo in my question—laughs brightly—stands up and walks over to stand beside me at the window. I feel her move into my space deliberately—feel her warmth, catch the faint odour of vanilla off her skin.

Always, she says. Your father drove me crazy with curiosity. He did it deliberately.

Olivia is so close I can feel the softness of her sweater, the firmness of her, inside it. I turn from her and sneeze so hard the fifties flutter across her desk.

I have to fish around in the glove compartment of my truck for my sunglasses. I agree with Olivia that if we are going to do this thing we should do it soon. But driving up Douglas Street I am filled with sudden anger. Another picture of Homer—white-bearded, spread-bellied this time—with his pants on. And alone—alone on his bony island—apart, hardly a factor anymore in any life but his own. Only he has this grin on his face as he writes. He sits and plots our lives like his next novel—reaching out to touch and control us into a future he dares us to defy…

When I get home the house is quiet—Bonnie still in bed—no sound from downstairs. I get the tape-swathed manuscript out of the box, bring it into the bedroom.

The splashes of colour from the crystals have moved down off the wall to the bed. The covers have slipped or Bonnie has kicked them away and rainbows move over her naked skin. I take the Swiss Army knife out of my pocket, open the blade and put it on top of the book on the bed table. I undress. Bonnie's skin is warm and smooth; we shift and murmur, adjusting to the fit of each other, hollow and round. In moments a thickening of feelings between us. Bonnie—more or less awake now—makes a face at me, but gives me a kiss.

How's Olivia Ashcan this morning? she says.

Very sexy, I say. But not as sexy as you.

You bullshitter. I've got to pee.

And she is gone. I lie there—my prick in my hand—feeling the spectral feet of the broken sunshine dance on my nakedness. The knife sits on top of the package. Fuck you, Homer. What will I find, if I cut that tape? Another letter, telling me you knew all along that I'd betray you?

The rainbow tongues of the broken sunshine lick me. Bonnie, in the doorway—naked, grinning. Aren't *you* a sight? she says. Then she sees the book, the knife.

Oh, she says.

I don't know what to say to that. The sun goes behind a cloud. I lose my erection.

Maybe I should leave you alone, says Bonnie.

No. Please.

I'm not going to make love to you with that sitting there, she says.

We both stare—the taped package, the knife. I am trying to decide whether to shove it under the bed or suggest we open it and read it aloud to each other—*while* we make love. The phone rings.

We hear Adam on the stairs, and then—there he is, big as life in the doorway. I'd almost forgotten he was still here.

Larry—you awake? It's Leila. She wants to talk to you.

Bonnie shrugs, pulls open her underwear drawer.

Mother's a little hung-over this morning, says Leila. How are you, Larry?

I'm fine.

Listen—I've got a meeting this afternoon. Can you drive Mother to the airport?

Sure—I guess so.

Listen, Larry. I think you should know I've hired Arthur Humble to find out what really happened to Homer. And to find his book.

You what?

Please, Larry—don't argue with me. He warned me not to tell you. Or anyone. Not even Duncan.

What on earth has got into you, Leila? He's a nut case. Artemis Hamilton?

His cousin? She set it up. She slipped me a note when we dropped her off last night. I met him at the inner harbour this morning. He said he'd been to see you, but you wouldn't believe him.

Wait, wait, wait—his cousin?

Larry—this is my decision. If he does find the book, it's yours—that was clear in the will. I don't need Homer's money, Larry. I don't know where he got it—I don't think I want to know. But I do want to know why he is dead and where his book disappeared to. Don't you?

For one moment I feel the nearly overwhelming urge to tell her what I know. I see a sudden window, opening in the ageless opacity of my relationship with my sister. I've always been stuck with being the oldest—if only by a scant hour. Our mother is not a large woman and I think we crowded each other from the start, even in her womb. If—suddenly—Leila has chosen to trust me, why not trust her? But...

His cousin? Look Leila, Homer wasn't pushed; he didn't fall—he jumped. An act of will. We may never know why—but don't you think we should respect his wishes? If he's dead it's because he chose to die—and if his book is lost it's lost because he chose to lose it. And if it should turn up, someday, it won't be because of Art Humble or his cousin Artemis.

You sound so sure. Maybe you're right. But it's my money, now. Not yours, or Duncan's or Mother's. Do you know why he left me his money, Larry?

No. Do you?

Maybe he thought it was the only way he could still hurt me, she says.

Olivia is still in her office.

Listen, I say. Do you think Art Humble is capable of putting a tap on this phone?

Possibly, she says. That technical stuff is the one part of the racket he *is* good at. You saw his idea of a disguise.

It worked on my sister Leila, I say. She told me with a straight face that Artemis Hamilton had put her in touch with her cousin—Art Humble. She then had the poor judgement to hire him.

Oh dear.

She thinks it's the right thing to do with the money Homer

67

left her. I don't like any of this, Olivia. Lying and spying and sneaking around. I came *this* close to telling her the truth. Or at least what little bit of it I know.

But you didn't. That's good. Be cool, Larry. I'll be in touch.

I pick my mother up to take her to the airport. Leila is up to something, she warns me.

I know, I say. She looks at me sharply and I know that already I have said too much.

Why do we all feel we can trust you, Larry? she says, echoing my own thoughts.

Beats me.

She's very upset about the money, you know, Larry. Though she's trying not to let on.

I know. She told me.

I guess I should be a tad miffed myself. All those years I secretly sent him money because I thought he was starving. What do you suppose he was up to?

I don't know, I say. Probably he took all the money you sent him and invested it. Olivia says he was a very creative bookkeeper.

My mother shoots me another look. Does she? Well—he *was* a cheapskate, except when it came to books. Books and booze. And you, Larry? You going to be all right?

Sure, I say. I've got Bonnie.

I'm so glad you appreciate her. Don't lose that, Larry.

Don't worry, I say.

I just can't really believe he's gone. Maybe *you* should write a book, Larry.

Maybe I should let you out right here and you can hitch to the airport.

Don't be like that. I always thought you'd be a better writer than your father; you are so much calmer—more centered—more truthful with yourself. I thought maybe that was what he was looking for out on his stupid rock. Some kind of inner quiet to the voices all trying to drown each other out—all his own voice.

I'm a good carpenter, Mother. I can build anything. I'm a fair contractor—whatever Duncan may think—an honest trades-man. None of the buildings I build in my life will have my name on them, and they'll all get torn down or fall down or burn down someday. I guess I didn't inherit Homer's thirst for immortality.

You're right. I can't imagine what I was thinking. Be a good carpenter and an honest person, Larry. But promise me one thing, please?

What's that?

No birds at *my* funeral.

Olivia sends me an airline ticket by courier. I put it in my underwear drawer, with the book. Bonnie finds it while I'm at work. Leaves me a note:

Larry, There's tofu thawed in the fridge. How long will you be in Ottawa? B

When she calls at five thirty-five I say, A day or two, at the most. Fly out—find the person—deliver the book. End of story.

So. Is Olivia Ashpants coming with you?

Yes.

Were you going to tell me that? If I hadn't asked?

No. You said you didn't want to know the details.

That's right. Now I *really* don't want to know. Are you going to fuck her, Larry? Was that part of Homer's instructions, too?

Don't be silly, I say. She's a lawyer, for God's sake.

Right. Look, Larry. Be careful, okay?

Always.

I tell Duncan I'm going to the mainland for a couple of days, Tim will look after things. Duncan isn't happy about it—neither is Tim. Tim asks me if Duncan gives him any shit can he crank him one. Duncan gets on the phone to Leila—then tells me she wants me.

What gives, Larry? I mean—we're all a little freaked out about what happened to Homer, but life goes on, right? Are things okay with you and Bonnie?

Things are fine. I've just got to get away for a couple of days. Tim can handle things here.

I'm not worried about the damn warehouse, Larry.

The night before our trip I get a call from Katherine.

I wanted to talk to you about the book, she says.

Silence at my end.

The book of short stories, she says.

Oh—yes.

You okay, Larry?

I don't know, I say. People keep asking me that. Maybe they know something I don't.

Look—I've got a manuscript put together. Do you want to see it?

No. Do whatever you think best.

It's a morning flight. Bonnie kisses me out of her deepest sleep—doesn't want to let go. I pick up Olivia at her office. Art Humble—wearing shades and a false mustache—follows us all the way to the airport in an old maroon Volaré.

Should I try to lose him? I say.

Olivia takes a small mirror out of her briefcase, checks her lipstick. It's perfect. Why bother? she says. He probably already knows where we're going. He's the one person who knows all about your father's secret life. You probably *could* lose him—but if you humiliate him like that he's liable to be a real nuisance when he catches up to us in Shawville. Remember, he's going to know his way around a lot better than we are.

I can't believe how stupid this is, I say. Homer is not only paying the two of us to fly thousands of miles to deliver a book we haven't read to a person we don't know—he's paying Art Humble to tail us. He's got me lying to my sister and my mother—and Bonnie wondering what I'm not telling her—all because of a stupid book. We don't even know if it's any good.

Your father, says Olivia, was perhaps overly fond of irony.

My father, I say, was perhaps a son-of-a-bitch.

We sit in business class; she lets me have the window seat. I stuff my pack—with the book in it—under the seat in front of me. No sign of Art Humble—if he got on this flight he must be in economy. Olivia gets a thick paperback out of her briefcase. The day opening up, blue sky in the west.

We may get a good view of the mountains, I say.

I hate flying, she says, opening the book.

I look out the window. I love flying, although it terrifies me. Maybe *because* it terrifies me? I feel extremely alive as the jet engines start to roar—very alive and vulnerable and sensitive. Aware of myself, my body; aware of Olivia's body beside me—close enough that I can feel her warmth, sweetly redolent of vanilla. She wears a smart blue suit with silver buttons and earrings. She folds her finger in the paperback and stretches like a cat. My father's lawyer.

Astrakhan? I ask her. What kind of name is that?

My husband's name.

Oh.

72

I've reserved a rental car at the Ottawa Airport, says Olivia. It looks like at most a couple of hours drive to Shawville. I've booked us a room at the Pontiac House Hotel. If things go smoothly we might be able to fly home tomorrow, but I've reserved the room for two nights, just in case.

The room?

She meets my eyes. I guess I should have told you before, she says. It's not my idea.

What?

There was a handwritten note on my copy of Homer's letter, she says. He said I should try not to leave you alone with the book, en route.

I see. How come I suddenly get the feeling maybe Homer didn't trust me quite as much as he liked to let on?

He said he felt it wouldn't be easy for you to resist the temptation to open and read it. He thought it might be easier if you didn't have to face that alone—I should have brought the letter— I could have shown you—

It doesn't matter, I say. I believe you. I just don't believe *him*.

I'm sorry—it's up to you. We can change it to two singles when we get there. We've got plenty of cash.

That might be a good idea, I say. Does your husband know about all this?

She looks me in the eye at that—a long, ironic, almost mocking look—then laughs and looks away. Otto understands that I have to respect the confidentiality of my clients, she says.

Well—confidentially, I say, Bonnie isn't exactly thrilled about this little trip. She's got some kind of crazy idea that I find you attractive and she—

Do you?

I guess that's kind of beside the point, isn't it? Remember? This is Larry, here—the guy who can be trusted?

She smiles and opens her paperback.
Good, she says.

The mountains are socked in. Already snow on the prairies. Olivia drinks vodka; I drink beer. They bring food, but too late, the alcohol has already taken effect. I use the washroom.

Olivia tells me about the first time she met Homer.

My wife thinks I've been unfaithful, he said. *Have you?* I said. *I don't really believe in faith*, he said, *especially not the blind kind. What about you?* I wasn't sure what to say. He'd fixed those eyes on me, and I knew if I didn't meet them he'd be out the door and find another lawyer. I was just starting out and I needed the business—so I met his gaze and said, *I try to keep my eyes open.*

Good line, I say.

It was true. Still is.

Sure. But you still ducked his question.

He'd ducked mine, she says.

Later—after another beer and another trip to the washroom—I notice again how beautiful she is.

Somewhere above the endless broken bones of Canada I fall asleep in a cloud. It's a warm cloud, which is good, because I seem to be naked. A young sea gull, perched on the wing above me, shrieks and flaps. Inside the airplane I can see Olivia peeling layer after layer of duct tape away from the book. I beat on the window, but she can't hear me over the roar of jet engines—the shrieking of gulls. She peels the tape away in coils—it gathers around her in a heap, slithers across the aisles and over the seat-backs—snakes around the ankles and throats of sleeping passengers who wake fighting hopelessly to free themselves. Olivia tears at the pack-

74

age—more and more frantically. The package starts to bleed.

I wake to the scream of consciousness. Olivia is asleep with her head on my shoulder, her fingers in her paperback, a faintly ironic smile on her lovely ageless face.

Olivia drives; I read the map, which is just a page photocopied from a road atlas. No trace of snow in Ottawa, but after we cross into Hull and drive through Aylmer and up onto a kind of low plateau near a place called Luskville, the sheer wall of the Gatineau confronts us, and snow gathers out of the grey afternoon. Big wet flakes explode on the windshield.

Olivia slows down a little. I play with the radio—find the CBC. Vicki Gabereau in Vancouver, talking to some writer. I find a French station playing rock and roll.

The snow is so beautiful. It always makes me feel like a little kid. I want to ask her to stop the car so I can make a snowball. Olivia is concentrating very hard. She's very lovely when she concentrates—but I think maybe she could still slow down more. I wonder if I should offer to drive, but I don't.

Don't kill us. Please don't let us die here—not before I get to talk to Bonnie again. How can she ever understand I never meant to die here, far away, in a rental car with another woman?

Snow gathers like fur. The wipers slap it aside but it piles in fast behind them. We see a couple of cars in the ditch. By the time we pass the turnoff for Quyon it is dark. Good tires on the rental car. Olivia slows down a little more. She is probably not going to kill us—and she is probably not going to sleep with me, even if I make a fool out of myself and ask her.

The first thing you see when you get into Shawville, after the sign welcoming you and announcing a pop. of 2000, is the sewage treatment plant. As we turn off the highway we pass a snowplow—a great steaming beast of a thing—going the other way.

We are alive—safe. She knows how to handle a car in snow. Her skin is perfect. She must be nearly fifty, but her skin is so smooth I can taste it. Maybe if I ask nicely?

I know I am fooling myself—swimming in my relief—as we pull in to the curb in front of the Pontiac House Hotel, but I don't care. It is wonderful to be alive, the snow is clean and beautiful; we might be in some alpine village. I won't bother asking for separate rooms; maybe they are all booked up, anyway—we'll *have* to share—Olivia steaming from the shower, perfect, all over…

I pull myself together and get out of the car. Grab my pack and the weight of Homer's book crashes through the roof of my fantasy like a bone. I crunch after Olivia, up to the front door.

The lobby is deserted, except for the front end of a dead moose. We follow the noise around to the bar—nearly empty at this early hour and filled with the wrenching strains of a jukebox steel guitar. Olivia gets the attention of the young bartender and he comes out front to check us in. I won't make a thing about sharing a room—they are obviously understaffed—don't want to make a fuss, an issue, look like a fool…

There was a mistake in our reservation, says Olivia, as the bartender riffles through the register. It should have been two single rooms—not a double.

He finds the page—frowns, smiles, shrugs and begins searching for a pen. Olivia hands him one of hers.

We don't get many in this time of year, eh? he says.

We'll be paying cash, says Olivia. Two singles—maybe next to each other?

She gives me an ironic glance, as if she wonders if I'm going to object even to this. I realize—with sudden, gut-churning conviction—that she is playing with me, that she believes absolutely that I will come crawling on my belly if she wiggles her little finger—whether we are bunking together or adjoining or in different hotels in different cities. This concession to my scruples means nothing, means less than nothing. It acknowledges my point—yes, with Art Humble on our trail, discretion might be advisable—but Homer has mailed us here in the same envelope and it matters little whether or not he licked it.

The bartender takes the cash—slides two keys at us and goes back to the bar.

Olivia has a sleek leather overnight bag, and her briefcase. I've just got my old canvas backpack. We each pick up a key and mount the stairs. We agree to clean up and meet in the bar in half an hour to look for some dinner.

The room is small and full of furniture. I put my toothbrush in the bathroom, hang my clean shirt in the closet, set the manuscript on the bed table with the roll of duct tape and the knife.

I run the shower a long time but it never gets hot.

Somewhere upstairs a man coughs, once, twice—then three more times quickly. Another guest? As I slip into my clean shirt he begins a long series of coughs—each gasping deeper, more desperate than the last. Thought we had the place to ourselves. A tubercular ghost? Some long-term off-season by-the-month renter, smoking himself slowly to death in front of the TV?

I calculate the time difference. Too late to call Bonnie—she'll be at work. I can still hear the shower in Olivia's room. Wonder if she's still waiting for hot water? Waiting for me? The guy upstairs starts to spit pieces of his lungs at the TV screen. I put my shoes on, put the manuscript back in my pack, look around for some-where safe to put it, then shrug and take it with me.

Hours later—a few beers under my belt—the manuscript in my pack heavy as history hanging off my shoulder—we stand, awk-ward, in the corridor.

You sure you are going to be okay with that? she says. A few vodka martinis warming the ice-water in her veins?

No, I say.

It's up to you, she says. She's wearing that angora sweater, so soft I can feel it from here.

No, I say.

She shrugs. I cannot be sure if there is disappointment in her sardonic smile.

Good night, Larry, she says, and then, as she lets herself into her room, she turns again and says, I think you are more like your father than he ever imagined.

She's wrong. Whatever I have in common with my father, you could put it in a thimble—still have room for ice. I lock myself in my hotel room with the feeling that I have leapt out of the path of an oncoming locomotive. Too bad I had to land here in front of this truck.

It is very warm in the room, though snow drifts in tiny dunes on the window ledge. I take off all my clothes but I'm still breaking a sweat. The man upstairs coughs. I turn on the TV without the sound. Fierce electronic colours leap from the screen to swallow the shadows. Two impossibly good looking people swim naked in blue water.

I take out Homer's book, toss it on the bed, place on top of it my Swiss Army knife and the roll of tape. In my shirt pocket I find a joint. It's been years since a stranger accosted me in a public washroom—and I never handled it well—but here, on the edge of some unimagined frontier, with sudden winter piling up in the street and Olivia holding court in the bar—the local men gathering around her like flies to shit—it seemed natural enough to accept a sample of the recent crop, offered by a proud farmer, even as we stood shoulder to shoulder at the urinals shaking the final drops.

I stretch out on the bed and make groupings. On top of the book I turn and rearrange the knife, the joint and the roll of duct tape. No pattern can make sense of these objects—there is no key to this puzzle. There are things that can't be mended with duct tape.

The man upstairs coughs and coughs and gasps for more air and coughs—chokes—spits. I can hear his phlegm hit the far wall. Homer used to cough like that after he took up smoking again, before he finally moved into the bookstore for good. He was already sleeping in the guest room most nights; I used to lie awake and listen to him fighting his own life's breath.

I wonder if Olivia can hear him, next door. I wonder if I should knock on her door, ask her—*There's some guy dying upstairs—I can't sleep—* She'll give me that sardonic smile, stand back to let me enter—but not *that* far back—not far enough that I can't feel her warmth as I pass...

I'd light the joint only I never thought to pick up a book of matches in the bar. Maybe I should go next door and ask her if she's got a light? Wonder if she smokes? My father's lawyer. I wonder if sensimillia makes her horny?

On the small screen, bronzed bodies leave blue water for white sand. I wonder if Olivia is watching this channel—wondering if I'm watching it—wondering if I'm wondering—wondering how long it is going to take me to quit wondering and get off my high horse and come knocking—on some lame pretext.

I pull open the drawer in the bed table and find a slim phone book, a Gideon Bible, and an ashtray. In the ashtray is a matchbook. I light the joint.

So it begins. They were foolish to trust me.

The smoke is profound, just as the farmer boasted. *I hear they grow some righteous shit out your way*, he said. *Here, try a hoot of this stuff—tell me if it ain't profound.*

Maybe later, I suggested, but he stuck it in my shirt pocket— winked.

Share it with the girlfriend, he said.

She's not my girlfriend, I said, *she's my father's lawyer.* But I probably didn't say it so he could hear.

My heart opens and swells to fill the space. I am minutely aware of every sensation—I feel myself—suspended—a sleepless

80

man entombed with a mummified manuscript in an airless oven of a hotel room—suspended—the bar downstairs, where they are talking about us—Homer's ghost upstairs, dying all over again, and danger all around.

The bud is fresh and sweet and smells like a friendly skunk; the joint is rolled tight and draws very slow. The room fills with smoke. I am a fish in the ocean of it.

What a place this is, the rear end of nowhere, though we're only just over an hour's drive from Parliament Hill. Upstairs Homer's ghost has finally gone to sleep. Or died.

Must have drifted off. Wake when my neighbor upstairs wakes in a spasm of coughing—choking—gasping. Have to use the bathroom. Beer poignant in my bladder. Must have left the light on in the bathroom. But what is Olivia doing in there—sitting on my toilet—nothing on but that angora sweater—rolling a joint?

Your thing isn't as big as your father's, she says.

I look down. She's right—it's very small. It stands, erect and eager, no bigger than my pinkie.

Excuse me, I say. I didn't realize we had to share a bathroom.

Through the other door I can see her bed. My friend the pot farmer is sprawled naked among her sheets. I really really have to pee, but Olivia won't get off the toilet. She has Homer's massive prick in a parcel, well wrapped with duct tape. I try to piss in the sink, but my silly little thing wants to spray straight up—all over the mirror…

I wake, in sweat, pissing myself—the sweet burning relief cutting through to consciousness like a wire. It is so hot in the little room I think before I am properly awake that the building must be on fire. I stagger to the window—struggle to hoist the sash, but it is painted shut. Outside the snow piles up like something happening on another planet.

I hobble to the bathroom door—pull it open—fumble for the light switch.

The toilet is plugged and overflowing. Duct tape and shit and print-darkened typescript swim round and round the bowl.

I stagger out of the bathroom—out of the hotel room, down the corridor—stark naked and squeezing my prick in my hand. I stumble into a public washroom—row upon row of stalls in bright blue tile. Olivia is there, in her nightshirt, brushing her perfect teeth. I try to avoid her, slip into a stall, but she fixes me with those eyes. I try to latch the stall, but the latch is broken and when I finally make it work I turn and find she has got in anyway and is sitting on the toilet—her nightshirt hitched up around her waist. I've never noticed how much she looks like Art Humble. Could be his sister. I try to get out of the stall—but now the latch is really broken. I really really really have to pee—

Which finally wakes me. I find the bathroom—sit in the dark—wait for the tension in my prick to subside enough so I can push it below the rim of the bowl and feel the brief ecstasy of relief.

I sit in the dark, still half-hard in my hand, listening to the sounds in the walls. Is Olivia awake, still—hearing me awake? Is she sitting on her toilet, or brushing her teeth, knowing I'm here—on this side—my prick in my hand, thinking about her?

I close my eyes and take down the wall. A simple matter—no electrical in it—just the plumbing stacks. Kick a hole in the drywall—break it back enough to kick the whole sheet off the other side. Olivia—her hair long and wild as the mane of a wild horse—stands, astonished. She wears nothing but a flimsy black nightie.

She's got her toothbrush in hand and she is foaming at the mouth—but she still smells like ice cream.

Lift her nightie. Enter her before she can spit.

Replace the wall—screw the shattered drywall back in place—tape it—sand it—paint it up nice before the lawyer brushing her teeth in the next room even notices she has been violated. A ghostly spoonful floats in the bowl.

Flush.

The blade of my Swiss Army knife is sharp, honed to a razor edge. The sticky fibers of the duct tape part cleanly, as flesh parts behind the scalpel. Inside the tape—more plastic, inside the plastic—a box. An old blue typing-paper box, soft cardboard, redolent of kelp and creosote and swollen full of paper. I lift the lid, turn it over on the bed. The pages are dry but wrinkly, as if the manuscript has been left in the rain and then dried too quickly by a wood fire. Two words only on the title page: **BONE ISLAND**

I turn the page:

My son and his girlfriend were making love in the basement. They probably thought I was asleep, and I should have been. I had the plans for my sister's husband's renovations spread out all over the—wait a minute, Homer, what is this?—staring out at the darkness like I expected to see—a parlour trick he called it. I've heard of appropriation of—wondering with half a mind what the fuck?

I relight the roach—smoke it till it scorches my lips then start again at the beginning.

I read. The voice is familiar, but it's not me. The style is

Homer Knee, I guess, but not a Homer Knee *I* ever knew.

He's got it all wrong, of course. The voice is familiar—well, *kind* of—*ululations?*—what the fuck kind of a word is that?—but the details are askew; the small ironies clang; I don't know this jellyfish Larry, and he doesn't know me. What he doesn't know about me would fill a book a lot thicker than this. But still—what he *does* know gives me the heebie jeebies.

And then I come to a place where I cannot continue. But I know I have already read too much.

I quickly put the pages back in the box and slip the cover on. A moment later I take it off again. I dig my fingers into the corner of the box till I feel the bottom. I get a grip on the very last page and pull it out of the box. I fold the page twice without looking at it and put it in my pocket.

I put the cover back on the box, wrap the box in a layer of plastic and reach for the duct tape. When I am done it looks much the same as it did before. I gather the rest of the plastic and used tape into a sticky ball, toss it in the wastebasket. Sudden mental picture of Artemis Hamilton—in a chambermaid's uniform. I consider venturing out to seek a dumpster or public trash can, but the snow has stopped at last—lies thick and perfect in the quiet street—ready to record every stealthy footprint.

I check the bathroom. I consider trying to flush it—but I remember my dream. I look under the vanity and find the access for a plumbing clean-out. *Bingo.* I unscrew the cover with the screw-driver on my Swiss Army knife and manage to stuff the incriminating mass into the wall cavity. I start to fit the cover back on—but I stop myself. I slip the folded final page out of my pocket and fold it twice more, push it into the wall.

Morning comes clear and bright, with a crashing of sun on snow that almost drives me back under my stone. For a few moments I am lost but I can feel the hard corner of Homer's book under my thin pillow. I reach out for my Bonnie, anyway, but she lies over the ocean. I come up empty—gulping for hope.

I get up, put the book back in my pack and find Olivia starting on her second cup of coffee in the bar. From a distance she looks perfect, as usual. But when I can see the whites of her eyes—they aren't, very. Maybe the friendly farmer slipped her something, too. There's a pot of coffee on the warmer; I fill myself a cup.

You don't look like you slept well, she says.

Guy upstairs coughing his guts out all night.

I slept like a log. I think the snowplows woke me once in the night, but that's all I remember.

I shrug the pack off, set it on the bar beside my coffee. Well—she says. I was giving odds you'd broken down and taken the knife to it. I take it I was wrong?

I let her take it however she wants. How many of those fifties does Homer have left? I ask her.

Plenty.

Then he can buy me breakfast.

I thought my guilt would ooze out of me like pus—but I detect no hint of ironic complicity in her. Maybe I'm not such a bad liar, after all. Hell, I've had plenty of practice. All my life I have been lying routinely—disguise and duplicity are natural states for me. I wonder what it would be like to be really, totally honest, once in my life? Too much of a shock to the system, I suspect. Don't even think about it.

Zanzu has her craft shop/tattoo emporium in a converted pig barn on the Seventh Concession Line. Driving north out of Shawville, the road dips sharply, then rises, and beyond the rise a dozen thoroughbreds stamp in the snow around a broken bale. Green and white hills to the north.

We find the turning—find Zanzu herself, in her skidoo suit, clearing the snow from her parking lot with precise strokes of a plywood scraper. I recognize her from a distance, in spite of more than a quarter century, in spite of the bulky skidoo suit. Something in the way she moves—I know it is her, even before she turns and I see her eyes.

Olivia parks in the cleared area, beside an old pink Parisienne station wagon. Zanzu gives us a single glance then returns to her shovelling. Go on in, she calls. We been waiting for you. The kettle's on.

Zanzu's shop is cozy, small, a single room panelled in barn board and hung with a variety of artwork—everything from the banal pastoral to the severely macabre. Some nice raku pottery in shiny iridescent black and purple glazes, displayed on tables made out of old telephone cable spools. Some crystals, some macramé, a few odd woodcarvings. Zanzu bangs her scraper on the logs of the building—the clinging snow falls away. She stomps in, unzipping and shedding the skidoo suit like a snake shedding its skin.

Come on in the back, she says, and tell me what the fuck you want.

She pulls aside a blanket and a couple of cats stick noses out, then retreat at the sight of strangers. The space we squeeze into is larger than the shop, but only barely, and into it Zanzu has squeezed her life. The tattoo studio takes up one end; the cook stove and kitchen table are in the middle and the other end accommodates a small desk and a narrow bunk. The place is cramped, but tidy, and very warm—the wood-burning cook stove hums and pulses with heat. There are only two chairs, and sitting in one of them, smiling vacantly and holding an unlit Camel cigarette, is Artemis Hamilton.

Zanzu reaches for the pack on the table, takes the other chair. I move to the stove, spread my hands as if to warm them, though they are already sweating. Olivia stands, holding her briefcase. Zanzu meets my eyes. The years haven't been kind to her. Her hair—always pale—is now almost completely transparent. Her hands are the hands of an old woman.

Artie told me about your old man. Bummer, man. I remember you a little—now that I see you. I sometimes wondered how it was for you—having him for an old man.

I remember you, too.

Olivia clears her throat. What a surprise, she says—icy— running into Ms. Hamilton here. A pleasure, of course—but the business we have to discuss is of a somewhat private nature. I wonder if it would be possible—

No, says Zanzu. Artie knows all about Homer Knee and his crackpot ideas. I could have had the guy in jail for harassment more than once—couldn't I, Art? No offense, she says—turning back to me—but your old man was a few sheep shy of a flock. I'm sorry he's dead, eh? I mean it's gross that the birds ate him, or whatever, but it's got nothing to do with me, eh?

87

We're looking for your son, I say. We have something Homer wanted him to have.

He ain't your old man's kid, you know. Sure—I took pity on the old guy, okay—I mean, like, I guess he wasn't so old but he *seemed* old to me then—I was young, right? He wanted to be hip, right? He wanted to be part of something he figured was going on—and of course he thought it had to do with sex. But I was already knocked up when I fucked him—okay? Y ain't his kid. Is he going to carry on with this bullshit, even from the other side?

She turns on Olivia. You're his lawyer, right? Well, you know what I think of the law? The law is a pig! She lifts the stove-lid and spits into the firebox. What's he want to give the kid, anyway? Money?

Olivia puts a warning hand on my arm—looking pointedly at Art Hamilton, all ears behind the stove. I don't care any more.

It's a book, I say. A manuscript. His last novel.

Zanzu stares at me blankly for a moment, as if I'd said it was a bag of shit. Then, gently, she starts to laugh. Art chuckles.

What's so fucking funny?

Zanzu shakes her head—drags on her Camel. My son, she says, doesn't read or write.

Zanzu stubs out her cigarette. Kettle's boiling, Artie, she says. Come on, Larry, give me a hand with a bit of firewood, eh?

The lean-to woodshed is nearly as big as her living space, and well stocked with split, seasoned hardwood. She loads my arms.

I don't trust fucking lawyers, she says. You seem all right.

People seem to trust me, I say. It might be a mistake. It's just a book, Zanzu.

She slams another frozen slab of maple onto the pile growing across my crooked elbows. What's a book to him? she says.

88

I don't know. He can use it to start his fire.

He just might. He's *deliberately* illiterate you know. He ain't stupid. Just strong-headed.

Did Homer know that?

How should I know? Your old man had this thing, eh? He was like totally obsessed. Artie told me he even hired this private eye to spy on us. He got this hard-assed idea Y was his kid and nothing would shake it, eh?

But you are certain he was wrong?

She doesn't hit me with the stick of maple in her hand. Fuck yes, she says.

If you won't tell us where we can find him—

No—she interrupts me, adding more wood to the pile, though it already cuts my wrists, piling it till I can't see her at all—it's the bastard's last wish—I won't stop you. But you tell Y the truth, eh? The bugger may be dead—but he's still fucking wrong. Tell him the fucking truth, all of it. You've come all this way, eh? Listen—is that too much?

I can handle it, I mumble, stumbling toward the door.

Back on Route 110 heading north toward Ladysmith. Snow blows across the road; stovepipes belch wood smoke. The trees come in thicker.

You don't have to go through with this, Larry, says Olivia.

I know, I say.

Talk about going from the ridiculous to the absurd.

Yes.

I can't believe the gall of that Humble character.

I'm coming to see that my first mistake was not to hire him at the start. He's very good.

He's an idiot.

For a time we drive in silence. We find the turn-off for the Old Mountain Road and follow it winding up into the hills. A couple of miles in we come to a place where the snowplow has turned around. Zanzu said we'd have to walk in from here. Olivia shakes her head and turns the car off. I open my door—drink in the clear cold air.

Olivia has a pair of transparent galoshes in her briefcase. She slips them over her little grey leather lawyer shoes. A jay screams in the bush. A clump of snow slides from a branch, lands with a muffled thud.

I break the trail. The snow is well up over our shins, melts quickly into my canvas runners. I tramp a ditch through the lovely smooth expanse and Olivia picks her way along behind. Here and there we cross the delicate trail of a mouse—the bunched pad prints of a hare—the crisp punctuated hoof prints of a deer.

The walls of the forest close; the unplowed road becomes a tunnel through the crowding, over-lacing branches. The wetness in my shoes works through to my socks and the ends of my toes begin to glow. We trudge past a small lake, frozen at the edges. Grey granite cliffs rising from the far shore. Olivia swears softly to herself, tramping behind me.

I stop suddenly and she almost walks into me.

Are you okay? I say.

I'm losing my toes, she says. If I'd had any idea, I'd have brought my cross-country skis. Are you sure about this, Larry?

Zanzu said it was about three miles if we stay on the road—two if we cut through the swamp. She didn't recommend cutting through the swamp.

Why would anybody live back in a place like this?

Because it's so breathtakingly beautiful? I suggest.

She stands there—staring at me—finally breaks into a smile. You're amazing, Larry, she says. In the brilliant light off the snow

I see clearly, for the first time, the subtle imperfections of the skin around her eyes and lips.

Let's cut through the swamp, I say.

The place where the trail leaves the road is clearly marked, but once we descend into the open marsh the trail becomes vague under the fresh snow. My wet shoes begin to freeze. Feels like I've got barbed wire wrapped around my feet. I step where the ground is too wet to have frozen, and sink in up to my sock.

I think this is it, says Olivia. She clears the snow off a stump and sits on her briefcase. She lifts one foot and slips her shoe off—tries to knead some life back into her toes.

What? I say.

Shit Creek, she says, and then we both look up because we hear the unmistakable snort of a horse.

It's a beautiful horse—a sleek roan mare—and the guy on her back isn't bad looking either. He is tall and young and sure of himself. He looks a little like his mother and a whole lot like Homer.

You've missed the trail, he says.

We noticed, I say. We probably should have kept to the road.

It gets even wetter, he says. Not a good trail without gumboots.

I'm glad you found us.

Rhona smelled you. She's got a good nose for strangers. He strokes the sleek neck of the mare and she mutters something.

She's beautiful, says Olivia.

So are you, he says. Here—climb up behind. I can take you through the swamp. I'll come back for your friend.

Olivia slips her shoe back on. Okay, she says.

I make a step with laced fingers and she puts her lawyer shoe in it and I boost her up. Y rides bareback, with only a blanket and a halter woven of baling twine—a single strand of twine for a rein. Olivia grips him around the waist with one hand—I put the briefcase in her other. Y makes a low clicking sound with his mouth and they are over the hill and gone.

It is too cold to sit and wait. My feet feel like they are made of lead—I clunk them against stumps and broken branches and the pain comes after, slowly, a molasses telegraph. I trudge on, following the trail of the mare, but keeping out of her tracks, for each hoof has broken through the fragile crust of frozen mud and filled to a little hoof-shaped pond. At last I get back on the trail, and climb out of the wetlands, but just when I think I am through the worst the open hardwood bush gives way to dense spruce and balsam fir and the trail closes down to a dark wet tunnel. No snow has penetrated here to light the way—I see only an expanse of mud and water, punched here and there by Rhona's emphatic hoof-prints. I can identify fragments of an old log road, but the logs were only sticks when they were cut, and now most of them turn to mush under my step. After a few futile attempts to pick my way along the edges—jumping from root to root—I resign myself and plod through. Every step sucks.

When I finally make it out into the light again, I sit on my pack and take off my shoes and wring my socks out. My feet are white and clumsy and stupid. I roll each damp sock back on and slip back into my muddy shoes. Knowing this dull numb stupid pain is nothing beside the exquisite agony I can look forward to when I finally have to thaw them out.

I'm trying to figure in my head how long they've been gone—how long till he should be back to get me. From what Zanzu said it shouldn't be more than a mile further. But he'll want to build up his fire, get her dry socks, blankets—make her tea? Still—by now they could have drunk the tea and done the dishes…

Maybe he doesn't mean to come back for me at all. I try to reconstruct things—the way he appeared, unsurprised, unquestioning—almost like he knew we were coming. The way he swept her up, vanished. Can it be that I have been missing the point all along? That the bundle of paper I have carried like a weight is only a red herring? That I have already delivered the true prize into his hands?

I am out of the bog, slogging my way through open hardwood bush again, when I finally hear Rhona on the trail ahead. Y dismounts.

I won't ask her to take both of us, he says.

I'm no rider, I say. Horses make me nervous—even with saddles and bridles and bits in their mouths.

All that stuff makes me nervous too, he laughs. Rhona's gentle. Just sit. I'll walk her.

He makes a step with his hands and next thing I am on her back. It's been twenty years since I sat on a horse, and I wasn't all that comfortable about it then. Rhona turns her head and looks me in the eye. She can feel the fear between us—an icy interface.

Relax, Larry, says Y. Olivia must have told him my name. I wonder how much else she told him? Y leads us up the trail. I watch for branches, try to hold on hard with my knees. We pass a derelict log cabin.

Hippies lived here in the seventies, says Y. They're all gone now. Some of them still own some of the land, but they don't come back much any more.

Do they know you live here?

Some of them know about me. I fix things up a bit. The hunters and mice and porcupines do a lot of damage. This was a farm before. The locals still call it the old Smith place, though the Smiths gave up sometime in the fifties, I think. Before that—back before the first big war—a man named Reilly used to quarry stone here. Look.

He shows me where the ruined walls of a round stone building still stand in places four feet high, so covered in moss and snow—with the forest growing up through them—that I would never have seen them if he hadn't pointed them out.

Sometimes, early in the morning, he says, I can hear Reilly down here, walking his horses in a circle. I can hear the grindstone—polishing the gravestones. How are your toes?

What toes?

Scattered around the clearing, large, lumpy, vaguely cubicle black objects hulk under a topping of fresh snow. My hives, he says. I just got them put away for the winter—straw and tar paper.

He leads us up a rise and back into the bush again. We stop finally in front of a peculiar little house made of two small geodesic domes, joined at the hip. A stone chimney sends a plume of smoke almost straight up. I dismount.

Go in and get warm and get a cup of tea, he says. I've got to give Rhona her rub-down.

A large screened-in porch built of cedar logs joins the two domes. A clutter of bee boxes and garden tools and plastic buckets. The whole place smells of honey. The door of the dome is pentagonal, and when I push it open I can feel the rush of warmth.

Olivia is up in the narrow sleeping loft, in Y's bed. She has a knitted coverlet pulled up over her breasts and a steaming cup in

94

her hand. Her clothes hang in front of the stone fireplace on a wooden rack. I set my backpack down.

You look comfy, I say, moving to the fire.

There's tea, she says. I'm finally getting warm. It's lovely and warm up here.

I strip off my shoes and socks. My pants are soaked to the knee, so I take them off as well, hang them beside Olivia's steaming jeans. The rush of blood back into my feet brings the pins and needles blistering up to the surface and I realize I am shaking uncontrollably as I fumble at them—trying to squeeze out the pain.

I didn't tell him anything, she says, except our names—and the fact that we weren't sleeping together.

Why did you tell him that?

He asked me. He never asked me what we were doing here—but he asked me that. I think he likes me. Larry—maybe it would be better *not* to give him the book.

What? Why not?

He seems so happy. Homer—your father wasn't a happy man, Larry.

If I don't give him the book—what do I tell him? Why the hell have we come here if we don't give it to him? If what Zanzu said is true—he can't read it, anyway.

Maybe it doesn't matter. He could be your brother, Larry. You don't have to hurt him.

I am in too much pain myself to reply. Fire ants under the skin of my feet, eating toward my brain.

Don't warm them too quickly, Larry. Here—see—the steps are cut into the pole. Climb up and get under the covers.

When Y comes in from the stable—grinning and smelling like a horse—we are both in his bed. Lunch? he suggests.

95

It is very warm in the loft. For a time I am consumed by the agonizing reawakening of my feet and toes, but eventually the pain subsides to a dull glow. The bed is narrow; Olivia is so close I can smell her—the real sweaty female smell of her finally burning through that scent of sweet vanilla she always wears. I can feel her warmth—a more exquisite, more poignant warmth than the background heat of the loft. Y has built the fire up to a noisy blaze and now, stripped to the waist, he hovers in front of it. He fries bannock in a cast iron skillet and warms a pot of his best honey.

Spring wild flowers, he says. We don't make a whole lot of honey this deep in the forest, but we get some wonderful flavours.

I notice he has no tattoos, at least on his upper body. Olivia sips her tea. I wonder what Bonnie is doing? Still early out there—she'll be in bed. Dreaming of me? I want to lie beside her and hold her and tell her everything. Oh Bonnie—have I slipped into Homer's skewed narrative after all? What am I doing here in this bed with this nearly naked lawyer? (Jerking off, probably, says Bonnie—without rolling over or opening her eyes. She's right, too. I wonder if Olivia can tell I've got a hard-on?)

Y passes us hot bannock and the honey pot. Don't worry about crumbs in the bed, he says. We can shake the sheets, later.

The sun dips into the trees; the long red light strikes the snow-laden branches from below. I watch the sky through a triangle of Plexiglas over the bed. Y puts the skillet aside and takes a penny-whistle out of his back pocket. He stands in the centre of the dome and plays and his music fills the space so full—it's like it's coming out of the inside of everything.

Y's music is like nothing. No apparent rhythmic or tonal pattern—each note held for its own sake—each perfect and poignant and alone. Then, when you can barely stand another moment of it, bleeding into the next.

Olivia has honey running down her chin. She chases it with a long tongue, but a drop falls between her breasts. She reaches for it with a finger—a fold of the knitted coverlet unfolds and her dark assertive nipple appears, commanding my attention.

The drop of honey glistens on the end of her finger for a moment and then she touches it to her tongue. She makes no move to cover herself, but she gets a strange look in her eyes. At first I think it is because of how I'm looking at her—and then I hear it, too. Y's music has changed—a soft, sweet, funereal melody emerging at last from the freeform jazzy flow of notes. A melody that has been lingering in my brain, coiling tentacles of song around my heart. Squeezing.

When Y takes the whistle from his lips and slips it back in his pocket, bends to check his bannock, I say, We've brought you something—it's there in my backpack.

Y opens the pack, takes out the rewrapped package. He hefts it, shakes it, squeezes it, turns it over in his hands—then lets out a full deep laugh that reminds me of my father and of my son. I bet I know what *this* is, he says. It's a book. One of *his*. Leo told me about him. Leo said he was a writer so bad even other writers didn't like him.

Olivia spills tea all over my erection. Her briefcase is beside

97

the bed. She opens it—pulls out a roll of toilet paper. Excuse me, she says. I have to use the facilities.

She climbs over me. Halfway across she encounters the damp spot where my erection used to be and we make eye contact—but nothing passes between us. Y hands her up her almost-dry clothes and watches her put them on.

When she is gone, he picks up the book again. I think she likes me, he says.

Homer's dead, I say. He was my father—Olivia was his lawyer. That is the only existing copy of his last book. His last wish was that you have it.

That's funny, he says. Not his being dead—but—is it any good?

I hesitate. For some reason, I say, Homer wanted you to be the first to read it. He wanted you to decide.

To decide?

Whether to destroy it—or to share it with the world.

No shit?

No shit.

I don't read English, he says.

You read other languages?

Not yet.

Didn't you go to school?

No. I couldn't. You see—I don't really exist.

What?

Zanzu—my mom—she doesn't believe in all that legal shit. She wanted me to live outside the law, so she never registered my birth. I know I was born in the back of a Volkswagen van, in the spring of 1970, somewhere on the prairies. If I *did* exist I would be a Taurus. But there is no legal record.

You must have *some* identification. What about medical insurance?

I don't go to doctors. I look after myself.

What about work? Your business? The honey you sell?

My customers pay cash—or barter. Nobody asks too many questions around here. The locals mostly don't speak anything but English or maybe a little German—the authorities won't speak anything but French. They don't have much to say to each other. It's a pretty good place to hang out if you don't exist.

We've made a mess of your bed, I say.

Y unwraps the package carefully, rerolling the tape as he strips it off, one wrap at a time. Probably he will use it again. At least we have brought him *something* useful. The process takes a long time and nobody says anything. Olivia has broken one of her perfect nails in the outhouse. She picks at it with her thumb.

When he finally has all the tape off he takes the box out of the bag and peeks inside, but doesn't open it. He puts the rerolled tape on a shelf, puts the box back in the bag and goes out with it. We hear the door of the other dome slam shut behind him.

I peeked in there when I came back from the outhouse, says Olivia. The whole place is *full* of books.

We hear the door slam again. Y returns without the manuscript.

It will be safe in there, for now, he says. What was our father like, Larry?

I am struck dumb by his question. Finally I manage to speak. Your mother said—

She's lying. Leo told me all about it.

Leo told you Homer was your father?

He said probably. He knew it wasn't *him*, anyway. He knew he couldn't have kids. Leo was married once—way back before he knew Zanzu. His wife left him when they found out for sure it was

99

because of him they couldn't have a family.

But Zanzu—

Leo made me promise not to tell her. I wouldn't, anyway. She'd probably kill him.

But how did Leo find out about Homer?

Homer hired some incompetent private eye guy to spy on us. Leo caught him lurking around one day. He made him talk.

I take a slug of my cold tea. I'm wondering just what kind of pressure Leo applied to Art Humble to make him spill his guts. I'm thinking I don't particularly want to meet Leo.

The other dome, says Olivia. It's full of books.

The people who lived here before left them, says Y. The hippies. You haven't told me what he was like—our father.

I don't know how to answer him. Who ever imagined words could ever be adequate for anything? Finally Olivia breaks the awkward silence. Your father, she says, was a very passionate person.

The brief November day fades and folds up under a sudden steel-grey sky. Any hints of a colourful sunset are quickly swallowed by cloud. Y lights half a dozen beeswax candles and lays another stick of maple on the coals. Snowflakes appear out of the night like little fuzzy bombs, explode against the skylight.

What will you do with the book? I ask him.

I guess I'll have to learn to read, he says. He speaks with a tremendous sadness. I hate my father—dead or not.

You don't have to read it, I say.

You didn't have to bring it to me, he says. When I can't come up with a reply to this he grins. Our father was a passionate man, Larry. We are his sons. I don't know what that means. I've never had a father. Leo was as much like a father as a bear is like a buttercup. I knew, a long time before he told me, that he couldn't be my father. I'm not sure I'm glad to have a father—especially a dead one. But I'm kind of glad to have a brother, Larry.

Y lays another stick across the coals. Snow falls thicker. I find I'm glad, too.

Zanzu always told me to live now, he says. *With your face in a book you can't see the sky*, she used to say. *Life is thin enough— you don't have to slice it so it will fit between pages.*

It is warm and safe and peaceful here. A good place if you don't want to exist. Anymore. For a while. My body feels heavy as wet sand, and as the snow falls thicker, till it blankets out the night—I let go. So easy just to let go. A good place to not…

My slumber is clear and dry and empty of dreams. When I wake, my bladder pulsing sweet fire all the way to my teeth, it is dark. Olivia is back in the bed beside me—the womanly smell of her now completely overpowering any lingering aroma of baked goods. I can feel the warmth of her, and hear her gentle sleeping breath. But I can hear Y's steady breath as well. Olivia has her back to me—her arms around him. I have to climb over both of them to get to the ladder.

It is still snowing.

Y says the snowplow won't come until the snow stops falling. The snow doesn't stop. We take turns chopping wood—feeding the fire. Y winds up his radio, tunes in the CBC. The forecast is for snow.

Homer's manuscript is somewhere in the other dome. I keep thinking about it, wondering what I really read that night—in that too-hot hotel room—what I dreamt? And if I really *did* break

Homer's trust, then why didn't I go the whole way? Why did I stop reading? What was I afraid to know?

On my way back from a trip to the outhouse, I peek in the door of the other dome. Olivia is right; it is heaped with books—hard-covers and paperbacks—literature and trash—mildewed, mouse-chewed volumes. I can't see where he has hidden the manuscript, but then, what would I do if I did? Steal it back?

Later, when Olivia visits the outhouse, she is gone a long time. I know she is next door, too, having a look, but something in Y's eyes tells me she won't find what she seeks. She comes back with Gore Vidal.

Tell me more about our father, Larry. Y stirs the coals.

I think for a long time. Something about the geodesic shape of the space seems to reflect time just a little—keep it from slipping through our fingers quite so fast. We all seem to feel perfectly comfortable in the silence but Y's request doesn't go away.

Our father—I say, finally. Our father who art in heaven... Being a father was a hard one for Homer to relate to, I think—I know he had nothing but contempt for *his* father. He never talked about his family much, but my mother has told me a little. Homer's father was a clergyman but he got into some sort of trouble—my mother thinks it was financial, not sexual. Anyway, Grandpa wound up in retail sales, then real estate, failed at both. In the end maybe Grandma's contempt got the best of him. He left. Grandma had to go to work cleaning houses to support them. Homer never forgave his father. Grandma was an artist—my sister still has a couple of her paintings. They're awful. My mother found her terrifying—and if you knew my mother that would tell you something.

In the forest, branches break under the weight of the snow. The gunshot sounds are quickly swallowed, muffled in the infinite white. We talk—Y and I—and Olivia reads, laughs occasionally, but whether at us or at Gore Vidal, I can't say. Y wants to know about Homer, and I tell him what I can. As I talk I realize that this process is telling *me* as much about Homer as it is him—forcing me to re-evaluate, to redefine all the vague mythical stuff that collects in the corners of family memory.

I tell him how Homer used to boast that he built a boat in his back yard when he was twelve years old and sank it in Seneca Lake the first time he took it out. That's in New York State—one of the Finger Lakes, I think. Homer was always brilliant, but he didn't like school. He was a rebel from the start, but he loved to read. He used to cut school and hide in the library…

When they drafted him into the army he knew he was going to die. He only hoped it would happen quickly, before he had to kill anybody. He was lucky. He never got anywhere near the front. An errant shell from his own side left him with a limp and enough pain to remind him and keep him drinking for a long time…What they call friendly fire.

Time suspended—almost. Hanging on heavy branches like the snow. So I reconstruct our father from fragments—a father figure. Later I leave the safe repetition of history and myth and venture deeper into memory and gesture—the way his heavy brows knit to a hard knot of anger when he felt trifled with—the way he handled his books—the way he looked at you—into you, when he spoke, even though you knew he was so caught up in his own thoughts he probably didn't even see you.

Later Y talks a little of *his* life, of the measures he must take to protect the delicate bubble of his non-existence. It seems the underground economy is alive and well in these hills, and looks after its own. I suspect something more lucrative than uninspected honey sometimes supplements Y's cash income, though he apparently has no use for mood-altering substances himself.

It's nice—talking like this. Was this Homer's real purpose

then? Was the book just a ruse—to bring us together in this way? Didn't he say as much in his letter? I remember again what I read in my hotel room that night—that long night that already seems so long ago—and I know it is foolish to try and second-guess the dead.

Later still, Y pulls out his pennywhistle again. His eerie drifting timeless notes braid strands of shimmering song into the silence. Finally, out of the bits of possible melody, he weaves a tune. That same tune, again.

That's a nice song, I say, when he finally slips the whistle back in his pocket and bends to the fire. Where'd you learn it?

Leo used to play it on his bagpipes, sometimes.

That's funny, I say. Weird—actually. That tune was a favourite of Homer's. We even had it played at his memorial service. Leo plays bagpipes?

Only when he's been drinking. He claims he played electric bagpipes with some heavy metal band in Detroit for a couple of weeks in the late seventies—but Zanzu says he was actually in jail that time for trying to roll an insurance salesman in a public washroom while an off-duty cop was taking a shit in one of the stalls.

Bad luck, I say.

Zanzu said it was his karma, he says.

You are welcome to stay, you know, says Y. Even when the snow stops. The stovepipe in the other dome is kind of rusted out, but there's a good stove in the log cabin. If you stay you could teach me to read.

It is the first mention of the subject since he took the manuscript and put it out of sight. We are real people, I say. We've got jobs and families. We exist. Our lives need us to come back and live them out.

It's all make believe, really, says Y. Your lives don't need you.

Bonnie needs me, I say.

Olivia makes a noise but I have no idea what it means.

You are lucky, says Y. Even if you *are* a liar.

There is a good stove in the log cabin, but we venture no further than the barn, the well, the woodshed, the outhouse, the root cellar. Y lends me a pair of rubber boots. Even just walking down to the barn, you have to watch as you brush past branches laden with snow. Most of the snow falls, the branch flies upward, and the resulting little blizzard fills your face and neck with cold sharp wet. Takes me right back to childhood winters in New England. Fresh tracks of rabbits and squirrels already filling up with more snow.

Rhona stamps and breathes mist at the barn door. Somewhere in the swamp a woodpecker booms away on a hollow tree. A good place if you don't want to exist. Time out of mind. Mind out of time…

Shit, I miss Bonnie. Wonder how she's doing? She'll be wondering why I haven't called. The snow keeps falling.

There is a good stove in the log cabin, but we sleep together, all three of us in the narrow loft of the dome—our mingled breath turning to steam as the fire dies. By morning we are clinging together for warmth. I wake with Olivia's knee against my bladder—an erection so hard it hurts. I clamber over them and down, fumble the boots on my bare feet, stumble outside to piss in a high twinkling arc.

It has stopped snowing. There are icy bright stars caught in the drift-draped branches. In the distance I can just hear the brutal scrape of blade over gravel, cutting across the merry jingle of tire-chains. The snowplow.

I go back inside, put my pants on, rekindle the fire.

Olivia slips me the rest of Homer's old fifties. Still quite a bundle.

I guess I'm going to stay, Larry.

You're joking.

No.

What about your clients? What about Otto?

Y is right. It's make-believe. I'm glad you've got your Bonnie, Larry. But my life doesn't need me.

I don't understand, I say. Are you staying for Y? Or for Homer.

You're right, Larry, you *don't* understand. I'm staying for me.

We stand at the porch doors, waiting for Y to bring Rhona around to take me back to the rental car. My pack on my back— light as nothing, now.

I've been meaning to ask you, I say. Did you ever sleep with my father?

Olivia gives me a look. Not exactly, she says. Homer was a passionate man—but he was kind of screwed up. Let's say he tried. You didn't even *try*, Larry.

The car smells of Olivia. All the way out the Old Mountain Road I breathe her blend of vanilla extract and desire, but when I make the highway I open a window to try and blow it out. I'm thinking about lost opportunities—wondering why I have such a sense of incompleteness…

All the way out to the car, with Rhona warm and forgiving between my legs, I wanted to say something—to warn him somehow. I couldn't find words which didn't sound mean or jealous and we tramped up the road in silence. But when we were standing beside the rented car and I was wondering whether it would be presumptuous to hug him or cold to simply offer him my hand, he said, *I may be only an illiterate bee-keeper, Larry, but I don't get stung very often.*

I hugged him. Solid as a tree.

I wonder how soon I'll be able to get a flight home. Suddenly it feels terribly important to be home tonight, to lie in the dark of my bed in my little house on Speed Avenue, with Bonnie completely close and breathing some kind of fullness back into the empty flapping skin of my life. I know now that all my eggs have always been in her basket. Was *that* what this is all about? Is *this* the lesson my dead father seeks to teach me? Hey, Homer—I knew that one all along. Didn't I?

So I don't know what makes me turn down the Seventh

Line. Didn't mean to. Don't know what I mean to tell Zanzu—or ask her—and I don't get to find out. The Tattoo Emporium is dark, the chimney cold, the Parisienne gone from the parking lot. I pull a U-turn and head into town.

As I crest the hill and look down on the village of Shawville —almost postcard pretty under all the new snow—I remember what it is that is really bothering me. It's that page I stashed in the bathroom wall. That whole feverish night seemed a distant, vaguely sordid dream, back there in the bush, but as I drive through town the memory is fresh as a wound. I know, now, that I did not read too much; on the contrary—I stopped too soon. As usual I have proven neither trustworthy nor brave, and now I am left with neither righteousness nor knowledge.

But the stolen page? What was *that* all about? Was that supposed to be the ace in *my* hole? Or only another nail in my coffin? Have I *always* thought in stale metaphors—or is *this* Homer's influence, too?

I pull up in front of the hotel. Okay. Get the damn thing back. Get it back and take it back out there to him, even if it means I can't make a flight tonight. Back through the swamp? Or shit—mail it to him. How do you mail something to somebody who doesn't exist? Worry about it later.

I sit there in the rental car in front of the hotel for a long time, aware of each minute as it passes. Finally I get out and go inside. The lobby is deserted, but the register is lying there, open on the desk. I take a look—then beat it back to the car, drive down the block and stop in front of a pay-phone.

I stand, listening to the telephone ring in my kitchen, thousands of miles away. Subtracting time zones in my head—peeling back the continent—too soon for her to be at work, maybe out shopping, maybe in the shower—let it ring—sometimes she just doesn't answer. Bonnie won't let the telephone rule her, but she won't let me buy an answering machine, either—because she hates talking to them. But why isn't she there—waiting, wondering why I haven't called, wondering if I'm okay? Finally I hang up. I've got to get a flight, tonight.

I phone the airline. If I make the airport in an hour, I can be home tonight. Driving again, I think how surprised Bonnie will be to come home and find me in bed, waiting for her. Or maybe I won't wait—I'll go over and surprise her on her midnight break. We can sit in my truck and share a cup of tea and I can tell her everything. Well—almost. When I tell her maybe it will all start to make more sense.

I'm trying not to think about my new brother, sprung full-grown from the earth, so handsome, so articulate—claiming such improbable, almost heroic ignorance. Or about Olivia, steaming in his bed. Or about Homer's manuscript or about the tiny bright scratches left by my Swiss Army knife in the tarnished heads of the screws that hold on the cover of the plumbing access—under the basin in the washroom of the hotel room currently registered in the name of Ms. A. Hamilton.

I watch the minutes flick by on the dashboard clock and I give the little four-cylinder engine a kick and try to pay attention. I reach down for the wild angry fearless part of me that held on hard to my father's leather-jacketed tree-trunk solidity as we chased death up all those country roads, so many centuries ago. I hold hard to the wheel—push down hard on the accelerator—only caress the brake, just a little, before I explode into the curve.

The only thing I have to do is stay on the road. Not think—stay alive—don't slow down—don't hit anything—make the airport in under an hour. Which doesn't prevent me stopping, once more, to stand in a bent and lonely phone booth and punch in the long version of my own number.

I let it ring ten times, even though after the second ring I can hear the emptiness of our little house—echoing as only emptiness can—all the way down the line.

109

In the airport, I am almost sure I see Art Humble, tying his shoe, but when I adjust my focus a little I see only a pop can recycling receptacle. I try Bonnie again—still no luck. I tell myself to relax; I'll be with her in a matter of hours. Even after I pay off the rental car and buy my ticket, I still have a stack of Homer's old fifties.

At the security gate, they look very carefully at my Swiss Army knife. They don't say anything about the duct tape, though I'm sure, in a pinch, one could hijack a jet with it.

I *do* like flying. Like being snipped out of time with scissors—suspended in a suspension of disbelief for a while—then hastily pasted back into the middle of a totally different collage. I sit between a nervous youth and a terrified nun. I feel strangely calm. If I sleep I dream only that I am flying home.

The first thing I notice—when I turn on the light in the front room—is that Bonnie has removed Homer's ashes from the mantle. Can't blame her. Probably shoved them in the closet, or down in the basement somewhere. Everything else is different, too, of course. The same stuff—but arranged differently. My desk is under the window; the love-seat is on the other side of the fireplace; some of the plants from our bedroom are gathered behind the computer. None of this, in itself, is unusual. Bonnie won't be trapped by patterns; every arrangement is subject to revision, and such inspirations are wont to strike her at the strangest times—in the middle of the night—in the middle of sex. After living with her for twenty years, I still have only a most fragmentary picture of the life she led before I met her, but I suspect she grew up in a house where the furniture was all nailed down.

Somehow, the very familiarity of this feeling of unfamiliarity is reassuring to me—proof that my Bonnie is real and herself unchanging. As always I find myself approving her ad hoc decisions. The light is much better there for my desk and I can keep an eye on the street. The love-seat fits in better on that side. The place looks great. A single brave late rose floats in a glass on the mantle.

I look for a note: *Dear Larry, I miss you, hope you are home when I get home tonight. Dear Larry, Why haven't you called, you big shit?* Anything—in Bonnie's beautiful free flowing hand.

No note. She won't be home for hours. Surprise her at her break or warm the bed for her?

I put the duct tape away in the kitchen drawer. Stand there drinking a glass of water—listening to the sounds in the house—trying to remember that night last summer, standing in this kitchen making tea for my father's ghost.

I feel suddenly, deeply, terminally tired. I crawl free of my clothes, still redolent of Rhona and the smoke of Y's fire. I sit on the toilet—too tired to stand and piss. It is very late now, in the Québec bush—they will be asleep, together in Y's crumby bed. I try to picture them—silent, breathing together in the darkness—but someone has left a lamp burning, and I see now that Olivia is awake, turning manuscript pages.

Our bed is unmade and smells like Bonnie. I sink into the lingering memory. I won't sleep—just rest my eyes a little and then…

I dream I am flying home.

I wake at the bottom of a very deep well. I can just see the fragile finger of the crescent moon—scrabbling at the well-edge miles and miles above me. I start to climb, pulling myself up, hand over hand—the fragile moss and creepers peel away from the rock, but I don't fall far, and soon I am climbing again.

The crook of the moon finally straightens to a spearhead of yellow light sneaking in at the top of the blind in our bedroom. No—it isn't daylight—only the jaundiced glow of a streetlamp, but when I check the clock it is so late it is early. And I am still alone.

It is four in the morning and I am alone. I get up, turn on all the lights. I handle the telephone. It is only six blocks from Osburn's gate to Speed Avenue—but at two a.m.—on a bicycle— a woman alone? She's been followed before—some jerk in a pick-up truck—three nights in a row before she turned and dismount-ed and faced him, screaming, five feet of fury armed with a bicy-cle. She never saw *him* again, but...

I put down the phone. In my heart I know this isn't about that. How did I miss the signs? There's her mug on the counter— the one she always takes to work. There's her bike light, for Christ's sake. She didn't come home from work because that isn't where she went in the first place.

I check the shed and find her bicycle. At least she's not out there on some lonely highway in the dark on her bike. This thought stops cheering me up when I remember her as I first saw her—face wide open by the side of a mountain highway—her thumb small and white in the feeble beam of my one functioning headlight.

I'm panicking. She's staying with a friend—with Lesley. She didn't want to be here alone, she was nervous, Lesley drove her to work—she forgot her cup. She'd never leave me, not after all these years, not just because I didn't call. All right, *maybe* because I ran off to Québec with my father's lawyer—but that was a mis-take and nothing happened—at least not to me—at least not like that, at least, I don't think it did, did it?

I pick up the phone again, put it down. I go through the

place. Her watercolours and brushes are gone from her work table in the music room. Her backpack, her toothbrush, warm coat, wool hat, mitts. Roughly half the cash that was in my underwear drawer—about fifty dollars. And her bear. *My* bear sits alone on the love-seat. He looks a little confused but that is how he always looks.

I pick up the phone again, but it is too fucking early to call anybody.

I picked Bonnie up on a windy night on a stretch of mountain road so lonely that the mournful country music which was all I could get on the radio almost cheered me up, a little. Bonnie cheered me up a whole lot. I was barely into my twenties and my heart was broken. I was running away from a woman who hadn't hesitated to use me. Bonnie wouldn't say what she was running from. She was almost *out* of *her* twenties, and she'd been running a while, already. Her energy filled my Mini from the moment I breathed the magic word—Vancouver.

I turn off all the lights and sit in the dark and stare at the even darker place where the phone doesn't ring. Finally I can't stand it. I phone Adam.

What's going on? he says, trying to wake up. Bonnie left this weird message on my machine last night.

What did she say?

Tell Larry to please not forget the plants.

That's it?

That's it. What's going on, Larry?

Nothing. She's left me. How did she sound?

Fine. That's the weird thing. But I mean—you know Bonnie. Are you okay?

Sure. Listen, if she calls again, tell her I'm back. Tell her nothing happened. It was all a bad chapter in a bad novel by a bad writer—and dead to boot. Tell her I won't kill the plants.

Jesus. *What* didn't happen?

I'd rather not talk about it on the phone. When did she leave the message?

Sometime last night. I was out kind of late. Dumpstar was playing the Malcolm Lowry Room. You sure you're all right, Larry?

No. Are you going to be around today?

I've got a class at eight-thirty. I'll be back later for a while. I'll call you if I hear anything at all. She'll be all right. She'll work through it, Larry. You know Bonnie.

Do I? Really? I know all those years ago when she shoe-horned her pack into the back of my Mini and fished a baggy of pot out of her underwear—I sure *wanted* to get to know her. I told her I could find her a place to stay in Vancouver, though the truth was I wasn't even sure where *I* was going to crash. We floated down out of the mountains—driving through the night—singing Dylan songs and then finding to our delight and amazement that we were both fans of the Incredible String Band. Floating out of the mountains singing:

> *Earth water fire and air*
> *Get together in the garden fair*
> *Put in a basket bound with skin—*
> *If you answer this riddle you'll never*
> *begin...*

I call Osburn's at 6:45. The guy who answers the phone is gone for a long time and finally someone else picks it up. She phoned yesterday, he tells me. She said she wouldn't be in for a while. Family emergency, she said. Everything okay?

Yes, I say. I guess we got our signals crossed.

Listen—we want her back.

So do I.

Okay. If she was going to call she'd have called. She already left me the only message she thought important. Don't kill the plants.

I consider killing the plants. I wonder about myself—when I get these thoughts. Then I realize that if she really is gone, I probably *will* kill them, eventually, anyway. Bonnie knows me only too well, damn it.

I sit wondering what the hell to do next, until I notice it is seven-thirty. I throw some fruit in a bag and go to work.

When we hit Vancouver it was daytime. My friend Peter was still at the same place just off Commercial Drive and he was up, getting ready to go to work. He offered us his shower and his bed. We slept together for the first time. I never touched her.

When we woke—in mid-afternoon—she thanked me for that.

I was dead tired, she said. All I wanted was to sleep.

Me too, I said, though—tired as I'd been—I'd lain there for hours with the yellow line of the highway still stitching the darkness behind my brain, wondering if she was really fast asleep there beside me, or if she was lying there wondering why I wasn't all over her.

I'm not so tired now, she said.

She was the irresistible object. I was the movable force.

Fifteen minutes later she was pregnant.

116

I park between Tim's pickup and this little red Alfa Romeo convertible I've never seen before—parked in the spot Duncan usually claims with his Dodge. Tim is inside, straddling a sawhorse, sharpening the stub of a carpenter's pencil down to nothing.

Hey, I say. What's with the red thing in the parking lot?

Tim snorts. How much bread did your old man leave them? he says, and then, If he calls me chief again—I'm out of here.

You've done great, I say, looking around. Any problems?

Just the one that's on the other side of that wall—sending faxes of his dick to the queen or something.

What's he on about now?

Doesn't care for the look of the seismic bracing. I told him there's lots of engineers in the yellow pages—maybe he should get on the phone and see if he could find one would sign him off for a blow job. I don't think he likes me any more, chief.

I silently invoke the earth to send *The Big One*, right now, to open up and swallow my brother-in-law. Nothing happens—so I consider removing the unsightly seismic bracing myself. A little dynamite or a D8 CAT should do it.

Tim seems to have things in hand. I go home.

The phone is ringing as I come up the steps. I rush—but when I feel the phone in my hand I know it isn't Bonnie. It's Leila.

Larry—Duncan said he saw your truck but you left without speaking to him.

Sorry. I forgot how sensitive he was.

Don't be a prick, Larry. What's going on? Are you okay? Is everything okay with you and Bonnie?

Everything is fine.

I'm sorry, Larry. It's just—she called me yesterday.

She called you.

I probably shouldn't be telling you this. She wanted information—about you and that lawyer.

I don't believe it—Bonnie called you?

Well—actually I guess I called her—about something else—but we got talking about you. She asked me if Art Humble was really working for me—she wanted to know what he'd told me.

What did you tell her?

Nothing she didn't know. That you flew business class and rented a car in Ottawa. That you stayed in a double room at the Pontiac Hotel in Shawville for one night, then—

That's not true! It was booked as a double—but we changed to two singles when we got there. It was a mistake in the reservation.

Nice try, Larry. You're a bad liar, you know. Arthur sent me a fax copy of the entry in the hotel register.

Arthur? Jesus Christ, Leila. Olivia paid cash for everything—that was Homer's instructions. The hotel clerk pocketed the difference, didn't change the register.

Get a grip, Larry. So you finally went and did something a little impulsive in your life. You're over forty, for Christ's sake—maybe it's about time. It's not like you're a serial killer or something. Though Arthur tells me you came back without the ageless Olivia. You haven't done anything *really* stupid, have you Larry?

You told Bonnie that? About the hotel.

I'm sorry, Larry. I didn't mean to. You know what a shitty liar I am. Runs in the family, I guess. It all just kind of slipped out.

I know what a shitty sister you are, I say, and hang up.

I will fly back to Shawville—force the bartender/night clerk to sign an affidavit. Which proves nothing, except that I'm so guilty I'm grasping at straws. But nothing happened—did it?—and isn't that supposed to be the bottom line? I'll go back there—I'll wear my rubber boots this time. I'll make *her* sign the affidavit. She's the lawyer; she'll know how to write it up. (Even as I imagine her there, pen in hand, attesting my innocence in longhand—I notice that she is naked under that blanket.)

Not a goddamn drink in the house. Okay—I'll go back there. But I won't even get them out of bed. I'll drip a little oil on the hinges of the door to the library dome; I'll turn the place upside down till I find the book. I'll read every word—at least till I get to the part about where the hell my Bonnie has run off to.

I take a bath, put on clean clothes, start a load of laundry. I check the plants. Good for at least a week, this time of year. There is food in the kitchen but I'm not ready to make myself sit down and eat it.

I start counting my mistakes. Number one—leaving Homer alone while I made the tea. I hadn't seen him for months. Why did I want to nurse the kettle instead of leaving it to boil and coming forth to squeeze my father's hand and ask after his health? But he knew me too well—he planned the whole thing. And yet I never thought he knew me at all. How could he? His own world was vast—if largely imaginary—and I was only one tiny island in it. But somehow he has captured me—distilled the essence of me. He sees me cringe from his embrace and everything else follows from there.

He feels more present to me, now, dead, than he ever did.

And that was just the first mistake. The others followed so fast I soon lose count—not realizing it wasn't a dream or a vision—not finding the book right away—not listening to Art Humble—listening to everybody else. Allowing myself to get close enough to Olivia Astrakhan to feel what it might be like to get even closer.

Agreeing to Homer's crackpot terms. Then breaking his trust. Then stopping reading—like some kind of dumb automaton—when the goddamn book told me I would. Though I was only just getting to the good part…

Hiding that page—

Thinking I could outsmart Art Humble.

Letting Olivia handle the money—pay for the room—make her sweet deal with the sleazy night clerk.

Saying too much in front of Art Humbleton at Zanzu's place.

Choosing to try the trail through the swamp. (Forgetting to bring my boots.)

Giving Y the book.

Coming back alone.

Not calling Bonnie. Letting the plants die. This last mistake—the only one I haven't made yet—makes me the saddest, with its implied inevitability.

I still can't help feeling I'm missing something.

I can feel the pressure drop when I step out onto the street. Speed Avenue is unnaturally still, waiting for the implosion. I drive by the job again. The little red Alfa Romeo is gone, so I pull in. But when I get inside I see it parked against the far wall.

The forecast said it might hail, says Tim.

How'd you like the rest of the day off? I ask him.

With pay?

Why not?

I don't mind. What's up? We going on strike for indoor parking, too?

Something like that. Better take your tools. Send Sylvie and the sub-trades home, too. Temporary shut-down of operations.

What do I say's the reason?

We heard it might hail, I say.

Duncan and I started in on each other the first time we ever met. He and Leila were already married. She married him on an impulse—none of us knew till after. She knew we wouldn't like him and we didn't. Maybe that's what gave her the impulse. But then, she was always attracted to assholes.

The first time we met he shook my hand like he had something to prove. So—Larry—the wood-butcher, he said.

I'm a journeyman carpenter, I said. I can build anything. What can you do?

I can see now that he was only trying to be friendly, familiar—to address me as he imagined we crude tradesmen would address each other. My insult was worse, being deliberate.

Leila laughed and said, Duncan has an MBA and he's very good in bed.

Duncan laughed too.

I feel a strange clarity. As if I really see and understand and am in control of what is happening in my mind. I have never, in fact, experienced anything like this. It's the kind of feeling I've often expected, anticipated. Falling asleep—confused and disoriented—I have expected to wake refreshed and lucid. Waking—still caught in webs of dream—I've *expected* to see things more clearly, to be capable of decisive, confident action, maybe after a cup of coffee? Didn't happen. I've drunk gallons—barrels—tanker trucks of coffee, expecting it to wash the windows, but it only thickened the sludge. I've ingested substances—I've waited to get off. Then I've waited to come down.

This is different.

Duncan looks up when I come in to use the phone, but he doesn't say anything. He's been on the phone to Leila. He pretends to be busy. I call Victoria Cement Man and ask how soon I can get a boom pump. Not till one-thirty. I call Butler Brothers and order twelve meters of concrete—with lots of accelerator. Duncan is running through checklists in his head and coming up empty. He calls my name as I'm leaving but I pretend not to hear.

I have almost two hours in which to reconsider. Instead I go to the Ingraham Hotel and drink four double whiskies and watch car races on the television.

I know I'm not fit to drive—but I do. My truck finds its way through traffic. The boom truck is already there, and one mixer truck. I hear another one exhale just around the corner.

Duncan is standing by the door, consternation stirring his features like a spoon. I ignore him, show Doug, the pump operator, where to set up. Duncan comes over but I point at his head.

Better get your hard hat, chief, I say.

What gives, Larry? Tim didn't say anything about pouring concrete today. Larry—but I'm already halfway up the big extension ladder. He goes and gets his hard hat. By the time he's back out I've pulled the nails on the plywood covering the roof hatch and Doug is swinging the boom with the big elephant trunk of the pump line—responding to my hand signals. When the end of the hose hangs down through the open hatch, I give him the signal to start pumping.

I can hear Duncan on the ladder as the slurry comes through in a diuretic rush. The four inch hose jerks and thrashes as the ram pump pounds the wet concrete through it, and finally the slurry thickens and heavy turds of wet concrete begin to splat onto the sunroof of the Alfa Romeo.

122

Duncan has his head over the parapet, but I am standing at the top of the ladder, so he has no room to climb off onto the roof. What the *hell* are you doing, Larry? Get out of the *way*. Let me off the ladder! Christ, have you been drinking?

I don't move. You were right, I say. That seismic bracing looks the shits. The way I figure—the only thing to do is pump the whole damn place full of concrete—fill her solid—then she won't fucking fall down no matter how much it shakes. Think I'm a little short on my concrete order, though. You want to go down and phone Butler Brothers? Tell them we need another four thousand meters of twenty-five mPa three-quarter pump mix, eh, chief?

We hear a ripping crunch from the warehouse below, which can only be the roof of the convertible collapsing under the weight of wet concrete. Duncan—finally catching on—goes white as a sheet. Somehow he makes it down the ladder. Halfway down he knocks his own hard hat off. He'll never make a fireman.

Duncan tries to say something to Doug, but Doug can't hear him over the noise of the pump. I wave my arm to keep the pump running and Doug shrugs and does. Duncan tries to get into the warehouse to rescue his car, but Tim has locked up securely. Finally Duncan flees to his telephone—but not before the driver of the first mixer truck blocks his way and gets him to sign a receipt for six cubic meters of concrete. I wonder if he'll call Leila first, or the cops.

Very funny, Larry—Leila calls me at home.
Glad you saw the humour, I say.
Have you any idea what that stupid little car cost?
Wait till you get the bill for all that concrete, I say.
I'm not laughing, she says.

Sue me, I say.

For what? You've only shot *yourself* in the foot, Larry. This is still a small town. Word will get around about this, even if we *don't* wind up in court. Who do you think will hire you to do a job after a stunt like this? And if anybody *does*—I hope it's not concrete work, because you'll be mixing it in a wheelbarrow with a shovel. The guy from the cement company told me to tell you that.

I don't know, I say. I've been thinking of taking up another line of work. Maybe I'll write a book.

Good luck.

You're the one was just telling me it was time I got a little impulsive. Anyway—I doubt if I've hurt my reputation all that much. There's an honourable tradition among tradespeople of getting even with assholes.

Are you calling my husband an asshole, Larry?

No, I say. I was talking about you.

Somewhere out of a dream my mother calls me.

Larry? Larry—are you okay?

Leila called you, I say.

What's happened, Larry? You were always the level-headed one. It's the book—isn't it?

What?

Leila told me about the book.

Told you what?

Really, Larry. I gave you more credit.

What exactly did Leila say?

She told me you had the book all along. I don't care what Homer told you—you shouldn't have lied to us. And you should-n't have gone and given it to some illiterate bush-child who probably isn't even really Homer's bastard. No good will come of it.

Nothing good has come of it yet, I admit.

I never trusted that lawyer, she says. I don't blame Bonnie for leaving you.

I was framed, I say.

I should have left Homer the first time he stepped out on me. It's very empowering to be the one who leaves. That hippie woman wasn't the first, you know.

I don't want to know, I say. And the kid *is* his bastard.

Leila said—

I wouldn't have given him the book if I hadn't been sure, I say.

I call and check flights to Moose Jaw, but I know she wouldn't go back there. Bonnie doesn't go back.

It is possible I will never see her again. No. Not possible. Adam connects us, always—she would never cut *him* out of her life. And yet—when I found her waiting on the soft shoulder of my life, she carried little luggage, but she left a life behind—left *someone* to lie awake and wonder. How do I know this, for she never speaks of it? Something in the way she doesn't speak of it tells me enough.

I wander through the darkened house. Missing something. Never did hail.

Bonnie and I always talked about cutting loose—pulling up stakes—striking camp and taking to the road, once our apprenticeships were finished and our son was out on his own. Adam has been living on the mainland for a couple of years. Maybe Bonnie got tired of waiting for me.

I check flights to Ottawa, but I know I won't go back there.

Adam calls me. Sylvie called and told me what you did to Duncan's car, he says. What the hell is going on, Larry?

I try to explain about Leila and Art Humble and Olivia and the bartender/night clerk. I tell him how Duncan climbed down the ladder and signed for the first truckload of concrete. I'm holding on to that receipt, I say, in case they take me to court.

So he's even stupider than he looks, says Adam. That doesn't help you and Bonnie. Listen, do you want me to come over? I can skip classes tomorrow if—

No—stay there. In case she calls again. I'll be fine.

Fine. Leila's lawyer calls me. I tell him if he's got something to say to me to put it in writing. He chuckles and says he's hoping that won't be necessary. Me too, I say, and hang up.

126

I'll be fine. My lifeline is cut, but I can breathe dirt—I'll be fine. My anchor is gone but I can bleed sea water till the oceans empty. Fine.

I watch the plants. They look fine but I know they are dying.

Events continue, on a cosmic scale. Planets rotate and revolve—everything in motion always—everything flying away from the place it all began, going where?

Jimmy, down the street, grows weeds in his attic. At first they lighten the air at the edges of my atmosphere, and the taste is sweet and profound, but after a while my pipe tastes like a road crew, the air is blue and my heart hurts. Drugs *can* help you to see around corners—but eventually you realize there is nothing there, either.

Every day heralds a new dawn. So what?

Sylvie comes by to cook me a meal. Like I'm an invalid or something. She is cheerful—she cleans out the fridge—stir-fries everything she doesn't compost. Too many onions, but I eat it. She wants to wash my dishes, too, but her T-shirt is too loose and her jeans are too tight and just having her in the house is giving me a hard-on, so I send her home.

Leila calls again. Listen, Larry—I've made you an appointment with a psychiatrist. If you will go see him, then I'm willing to forget the loss on the Alpha Romeo. You'll still have to clean up that mess at the warehouse, Larry—of course—but hopefully we can still complete the project on schedule. My lawyer thinks I'm crazy to take the loss on the car—he thinks they should send you to jail, but my first concern is for *you*, Larry. I know how upset you are—I know you think you hate me, but I only want you to think about yourself and our mother and Bonnie and Adam and please go see this guy. He's supposed to be good for problems like yours...

That's a good one.

Maybe he can help you, Larry.

Sure. Like all those shrinks helped you.

They *did* help me, Larry. Or maybe you would rather I'd stayed in that place.

Maybe.

Please, Larry.

I thank her for her concern—her generosity of spirit. I make her repeat the psychiatrist's name and address, slowly, so she will think I am writing it down, though actually I am not even listening.

In the dark parts of the night I lie with my eyes open and walk through the house in my mind, seeking the clue I know must be there. She would not go without leaving me a message—so how come I don't get it? I feel immensely stupid, profoundly incapable of connected thought. I remember a moment of clarity, I think. But probably it's a false memory, for hasn't science proven recently that moments don't exist—can't exist? Besides—look where it got me.

Somewhere between the day and the night I turn on the computer—try to write my own version—the unvarnished truth:

When I was fourteen my father grew a beard and bought a motorcycle. We were Americans, then, all except my mother, who came from Montreal. It's funny, because we are all Canadians, now, except my mother. We lived in a white house with green shutters in the Berkshire Hills of Massachusetts, not far from the New York state line.

My mother taught in a private school. Homer was working on his fourth novel (or was it his third?) He'd almost sold one to a New York publisher, but they wanted him to change the ending.

One summer, Homer took me on the back of his motorcycle, across the state line, to watch a bunch of bands play rock and roll in a field. It rained. All the gods pissing at once. My sister was mad we didn't take her.

I remember every twist and turn of those mountain roads, my skinny arms wrapped tight around Homer's leather-jacketed waist, eating bugs and holding on for much more than dear life. Not afraid to die, only to let go…

I read over what I have written, then turn off the computer without saving the file.

Katherine calls.

Larry? How's it going?

She sounds almost cheerful, and not particularly concerned with how it is going. I realize—with a shock—that she still knows nothing of all that has passed since Homer's memorial. I try to pay attention.

Okay, I say. How are you?

Living. Listen—I've got good news. I put together that book of stories I was talking about, showed it to somebody I know who works for this small press on the mainland. She just called to say they love it. They want to fast track it for the spring list.

You're joking.

No. I'm going over to talk details tomorrow. Since you own the copyrights I thought you should be there.

I'm busy tomorrow. I trust you.

It won't be much of a print run, of course. It's just a small press, but they *do* have national distribution, and they *have* won a few awards. The advance won't amount to much, either, I'm afraid.

Too bad. I could use a windfall. My sister is suing me.

What?

It's a long story.

But he left *her* all that money. Why is *she* suing *you*?

I've been doing some work for her husband. We had a small disagreement regarding the placement of some concrete.

Jesus.

I don't get it, Katherine. Why is Homer's work suddenly a hot prospect? Because he's dead?

It helps, I'm afraid. I told them the whole story. They got pretty excited when I told them about the lost book. A little tragedy, a little mystery—it's amazing how Homer's twisted little stories take on a more profound edge when you know the tragedy they presaged.

I think it's sick, I say. All his life publishers scorned him—or damned him with faint praise—pushed his manuscripts to the back of the desk, the bottom of the pile. He lies down and dies and suddenly he's on the fast track to the spring list.

You're right, Larry, she says. It sucks. But I just don't know what else I can do for him.

I call Olivia's office. They tell me she's on stress leave.

I find Otto Astrakhan in the phone book. I dial the number—don't identify myself. Have you heard anything from

130

Olivia? I ask.

Who is this?

Someone, I say.

After a brief silence he says, I haven't heard from Olivia in years. We were divorced in 1974.

The mailperson brings Bonnie's Record of Employment from Osburn's, with a note, wishing her good luck.

My mother calls again. I tell her Katherine's news.

All the more reason to get the novel back from that illiterate creature, she says.

You're talking about my brother, I say.

Half-brother at the very most, Larry. And considering how you and your twin sister have been behaving lately, I guess blood isn't a hell of a lot thicker than dishwater—not in *this* family.

Leila calls. You missed your appointment, Larry.

Tell Art Humble I want to talk to him.

Arthur hasn't been able to find your Bonnie yet—if that's what you want to know.

Has he been looking for her?

Of course. I'm on *your* side, Larry. God knows why. I made you another appointment.

Make him stop.

What?

Make him stop looking for her. Now.

But Larry—

Call him off, Leila. The concrete in the car was stupid. I'm sorry. Call off your fucking detective.

Don't threaten me, Larry.

I didn't threaten. I apologized.

It sounded like a threat. Are you going to keep the appointment, Larry?

No.

Duncan is hardly speaking to me. He thinks I shouldn't even be talking to you.

So why *are* you?

God knows—

She hangs up on *me.*

I try the computer again:

Speed Avenue is quiet, sulking in shadow. How have I come so far from where? Is this person really me, who always had a lover? Who is this suddenly loverless person pretending to be? Me?

I get it. All is lost. I bridle.

Speed Avenue is quiet, sulking. No one is making love. My father's ghost comes tramping up the steps onto the porch and peers in the window.

He sees that Bonnie has rearranged the furniture, again. She's moved his ashes from the

I turn off the computer. I call Sylvie and ask her if she will look after the plants.

A man alone in his truck. A man, alone in his pickup truck on a logging road to the back of the beyond. A man. Alone.

Homer got the map in trade from a one-legged drug smuggler—he gave the guy his autographed first edition of Roderick Haig-Brown's *A River Never Sleeps* for it. They were both drunk as pirates; it was a long time ago. I remember Homer told me the guy had the strangest eyes, like you could see flames reflected in them.

The map didn't exactly show where Bone Island was to be found—it was more allegorical—but it did eventually lead to the camp of a Nuu-chah-nulth elder named Margaret, who owned a good boat and knew the treacherous waters and the way.

In those days Homer always had a bottle of Irish whiskey in the bottom drawer. He'd already had a couple before the smuggler wandered in, pockets full of unlaundered bills, on the run from somebody he'd thought he could trust. The smuggler had had a couple, too—at the King Eddie—couldn't find his car. He came in to use the phone, only Homer didn't have one. Homer was re-reading the Haig-Brown, which had been given to him personally by the author. The smuggler wanted it badly—he piled twenties on the table but Homer only laughed and put the book in the bottom drawer and took the bottle out.

The bottle was nearly full when they started it. By the time they finished it, Homer had traded that treasured, personally inscribed first edition for a geographical allegory scrawled in pen-

cil on a piece of yellow foolscap by a wanted criminal too drunk
to stand up.

Bone Island isn't even always an island. At the very lowest of
tides it is more of a peninsula—a jagged elbow of rock, a few
stubborn fir trees and that one wind-blasted pine. But it shelters
a tiny harbour—if you know what you are doing you can beach a
boat there, even in hard weather. That yellow foolscap map was
the only title Homer ever had to the place, which the smuggler
never owned to barter. Even Margaret doesn't know who origi-
nally built the tiny shack up under the overhanging rock. It had
been empty for years when the smuggler and his partners took it
over—tightened it up and made use of it as an off-loading station.
Homer had that map some more years before he found his way
there. His first visit was brief, but he came back, and each time he
came he stayed longer.

But Homer is dead. I am alone—a man alone in his pickup,
beyond the beyond of beyond—beyond the slash and burn,
beyond belief and disbelief and on and on beyond—beyond the
washouts and the washboard rattling teeth in my skull, beyond
the rock-slides and the roadkill—it is long dark when I find the
final turn to the last rough stretch of road to Margaret's camp.

It is raining gently—the road is mud. At the bottom of the
last big hill my way is blocked. Art Humble—up to his ankles in
muck—is crying on his Volaré.

He is wet through to the skin, muddy to the knees and when
he sees me he gets back in the car, which is mired to the axles. He
won't open the window. I shrug and push him out with my truck.
As soon as he feels the road under his wheels he floors it. I follow
more cautiously and at the last hairpin turn I find him well and
truly in the ditch.

I wait in my truck as Arthur climbs out the passenger side
window and fights free of the dense salal. I roll down my window.

Need a ride, Arthur?

No thanks.

For Christ's sake, man. You're going to need a tow truck—maybe a crane—to get that baby out of there. Get in.

He bites his lip, brushes at the mud that specks his trousers, kicks some of the mud off his running shoes and gets in.

Thanks, he says.

What are you doing out here, Humble?

Following up a lead.

You don't seem real familiar with the road.

I never came this way before. Too risky. My business with your father was at arm's length.

Homer had pretty long arms, I say.

Listen, he says. I didn't mean for this to happen.

For what to happen?

Your wife leaving you. Because of my report about you and that lawyer.

My wife hasn't left me. And if she did it wouldn't be because of you. Listen—Humble, I've been thinking. It was a mistake to let you go to work for my sister. Whatever she's paying you—I'll double it.

Should have pulled the plates on that car. Shit.

Forget the car. I want you to tell me everything.

What are you talking about?

The dogs welcome us to Margaret's camp. Familiar smells of fish and wood smoke. Margaret lives alone in a tiny cabin but various of her children and grandchildren live seasonally in a collection of campers between her garden and her wharf. Margaret has a low fire in her barrel stove, a pot of tea strong as a steel cable.

She said you would come, she says.

Is she okay?

Margaret shrugs. You'll sleep here. The tide turns just after dawn. I'll run you across before breakfast.

Thanks, Margaret. This is Art Humble. He had a problem with his car.

Margaret gives Arthur a blanket and he undresses under it. She hangs his wet muddy clothing behind the stovepipe. She gives us smoked salmon and hard bread.

I told your father, the first time he showed up here, on that motorcycle—*Bone Island is nothing but grief.* He laughed at me. He was cute in those days—before he grew so much belly. I told him—*Look what happened to those smugglers.* He didn't know about that.

What happened to them?

Nobody knows. All they found was their shoes.

Margaret makes up a bed for us between the stove and the pantry door. Arthur has a toothbrush with him—I've forgotten mine. When Margaret kicks out all the dogs but one and blows out the kerosene lamp, the fire makes maps of bloody rivers on the walls and ceiling. I can still feel the washboard, see the endless hectares of clear-cut slash, but Art—anonymous, androgynous Art—is pretending to snore.

I wake suddenly, in total dark. The fire is out and I can feel the cold suck under the pantry door. I am alone in the bed. Bladder full—penis erect—I feel my way across the room to the door and stagger out under the stars.

The sky is clear, each star edged in crystal. The moon sets into an ocean calm and thick as syrup. Down by the wharf I can see someone putting something into Margaret's boat. I run down the hill—but as I run I notice that my feet are not touching the

136

ground—I am moving very slowly—I begin to suspect that I may be only dreaming…

I wake to find the stove cold, Art Humble snoring for real, my dick hard as oak, my bladder sending messages to my teeth. In the almost dead dark, Arthur's sleeping face is innocent and childlike, and perfectly androgynous. It occurs to me to pull back the blanket and see if it is *really* Arthur—or actually Artemis, but when I do I find instead that it is actually Olivia—naked as mother nature—her nipples dark and hard as chocolate drops—her knees invitingly wide. I climb her like a mountain, but I can get no traction in the deep softness of her flesh—I begin to slip…

I wake pissing myself. My bed partner is crowding me. I stagger outside and piss off the cliff.

I wake to the sound of Margaret lighting the fire. Art Humble is gone.

Out behind the shed, burying his licence plates, says Margaret. We'll have tea, then go.

It is raining, gently; the wind is light but steady; the swells are low. Slack tide. We round a headland and the sky crowds lower, but Margaret knows every rock. Art Humble crouches in the bow, trying to look cool.

They said he died drinking whiskey—Margaret speaks softly, so Arthur, in the bow won't even know she's spoken.

They found the empty bottle beside him, I say.

He never got it from anybody at my place.

He brought it from the city, I say. He was down there—just before. He came to see me.

She looks at me skeptically but says nothing. For a long time nothing but the sea and the fog and the screams of a single following gull. When Bone Island suddenly looms out of the fog—I shiver.

Might've been that other one brought it, she says, suddenly.

The other one? You mean Katherine.

No. That other one—last spring he come around.

Who? Did he have a name? What did he look like?

Big white man with a beard. Claimed he was your father's brother, but I knew he lied.

Homer didn't have any brothers or sisters, I say.

Too bad, she says.

Most of Bone Island is still under the elbow of the fog, but as we slip between the rocks which shelter the tiny pebble beach, I catch a glimpse of Homer's shack crowded up under the sheltering rock. I look for Bonnie's face at the door or window. She must have heard our motor—but the place is still, except for a smear of muddy wood smoke streaking the shimmering fog.

Art Humble stands on the beach, his hands in his pockets, looking like he wishes he smoked so he could light up. Margaret sets a red gas can on a rock, well above the high tide line. She gestures to Homer's flat-bottomed aluminium skiff, pulled up between two boulders, covered with a blue tarp.

Wait for slack tide, she says. Follow the points till you see my smoke. That's a good little motor—your father bought it from my grandson. She'll start up—no problem.

I give her one of Homer's fifties, folded twice. She slips it in

138

her boot.

Look, says Arthur. I guess I may as well go back with Margaret. You and your wife will probably want some time to make things up. She isn't going to want to see *me*.

You're right, I say. But I'm not letting you out of my sight till I get a few answers. And till you tell her a couple of things about what you did and did not find out in Québec.

You aren't my boss. I never said I'd work for you—Margaret yanks on the pull-cord and her outboard grumbles back to life. Look, I could wait for you back there, he says, almost pleading. My car's in the ditch—where am I gonna go? Even as he speaks, Margaret's boat is pulling away from the beach. Okay—he says, watching Margaret carefully nose her way into the narrow channel. Okay, I'll work for you. But there are things it's better you don't know. That's what I told your sister, too.

Right, I say. Those are exactly the things you are going to tell me—later. Wait here till I call you.

Art pushes his hands deeper in his pockets, shrugs, sits on a rock. Margaret lifts a hand and she is out of sight. I leave Art Humble there on the shore and scramble up the steep rocky path to find Bonnie.

A crooked little shack—built of split cedar flotsam—jammed up under the backbone of the island. It looks much the same as it looked the first time I saw it more than ten years ago. *There was a crooked man, who built a crooked house,* I think, as I thought then, but again I marvel at how any construction so skewed and arbitrary in design could withstand the brutal assault of the storms which blast this coast.

Bonnie *must* have heard Margaret's motor—our voices— but she still doesn't show. I hesitate in front of the door, move to the small window, but it is so grimed with salt I can make out nothing. I wonder if I should knock, or call out, but finally I just push the slab door open.

Bonnie is in Homer's big chair, her back to me, her feet to the stove. She doesn't turn to look at me. Homer's urn on the floor beside the chamber pot.

Hi, Bonnie.

She turns and looks at me then, but her expression is empty, distant, and she turns back at once to the fire.

Did you bring anything to read? she says.

I thought Homer was the world's biggest book freak, says Bonnie. This place used to be *full* of books, didn't it? What did he do with them all? There isn't a damn pamphlet on the whole island. Not even a cookbook. Isn't that weird?

Yeah, I say. But then, I just came back from visiting my half-brother who can't read or write—and half his house *is* full of books. We're a strange family.

Oh, yeah, she says. How was your trip? Did you get to fuck that lawyer?

No.

Poor Larry.

I tried to call you. There's no phones out there. We got snowed in—very unusual weather for this early in the year.

Did she turn you down or was it your scruples? Or is that an unfair question?

Yes, I say.

Yes which?

Yes to all three.

She laughs, but she still doesn't turn to look at me. I dumped the can, she says, gesturing vaguely with her thumb. I think first she means the chamber pot but then I see she is actually indicating the urn. Sorry—I couldn't wait, she says. I don't know what was in it—but it wasn't Homer.

What?

It wasn't him.

What do you mean? Why do you say that?

Because he isn't dead, she says.

I walk around the stove till I am facing her, but her eyes stay with the fire. She sits in Homer's big chair like a small child, holding her bear to her heart. I saw him, she says.

You saw him? Alive? Here? On the island?

I know. I've tramped over the place a dozen times in the daylight. If he's got a hiding place—it's a hell of a good one. Maybe he comes over by canoe or something. Maybe he wades across at low tide—it was the middle of the night—he had his rubber boots on.

What did he say? What did he do?

I'd rather not talk about it.

Jesus. You're sure you weren't dreaming?

Fuck you, Larry, she says—finally looking at me, through me.

I'm sorry. I just don't—What did he *do* to you?

He didn't *do* anything to me. I said I don't want to *talk* about it, okay?

Homer isn't dead. You saw him here, alive. But you don't want to talk about it.

Don't get mad at me, Larry. I haven't had a very good time.

I swear if he *is* alive—if this is all some kind of joke—I'll— I'll—I'll kill him myself.

I don't know, Larry. Maybe you're right. Maybe I *was* dreaming. Maybe it *was* a ghost. I was ready to think that the next morning. That's why I dumped the ashes. I went right out on the point and chucked them. But it wasn't him. I was listening, see, for that piece of shrapnel from his knee—for the ring of it, on the rock. But it was just ashes and dust.

Yeah, well, he could have made *that* story up, too. I know my mother had her doubts.

You think I'm crazy, don't you? You think I've gone off the rails—that losing you to that bitch lawyer was too much for me.

I don't think you're crazy. I don't know what to think. I mean, if Homer *was* alive it might explain a few things. Like how he put a whole lot of stuff in his so-called novel that hadn't *happened* yet when he died. But if he *is* alive, then who *was* in that bag the Mounties gave me? And what about the dental records? The X-rays. The Coroner's office made a positive I.D. from the X-rays.

I don't know, Larry—is Margaret coming back for us?

No—she left us gas for Homer's boat, I say—but even as I speak I hear what Bonnie has heard—the spluttering sound of an outboard down at the harbour. I yank open the narrow door and stumble out into the light in time to watch Homer's little skiff disappear into the fog—Art Humble crouched over the outboard, feeling his way among the rocks.

It takes me a while to explain to Bonnie how I have managed to get us marooned together on Bone Island. She looks at me like she can't believe she never noticed before what an unrestrained idiot I am. For some reason this prompts me to rave on and before long she knows all about Leila and about Duncan's car and she looks at me like all this only confirms her suspicions. I go on and on—working my way backward till she knows about Y and Olivia—and finally I tell her about the book.

You read it after all, she says.

Only part of it, I say.

God, Larry. Can't you ever, once in your life, do something the whole way?

I love you, I say. The whole way.

Yeah, she says, but maybe it would have been better if you *had* fucked that lawyer.

Sitting here, the stove beating hot between my knees, I can swear I smell my father—I can almost believe he is alive. Bonnie has a pot of coffee keeping warm on the foot-plate, but she doesn't offer me any. I still don't get why you wanted to bring that creep here in the first place, she says.

I thought maybe I could make him tell me what he really knows about Homer.

Jesus, you just can't let go, can you, Larry? And what if he *did* tell you something? Would you believe him? *I've* told you something, and you don't believe *me*. I can tell you something else, too. I was wondering if you were going to come. I said to myself—*it doesn't matter, as long as he comes.* Then I said—*no, it* does *matter, but it'll be okay as long as he comes, as long as he doesn't bring her.* I guess I was wrong.

I'm sorry. I blew it.

Yeah.

If Arthur went back to Margaret's—she'll know we're stuck. She'll probably bring the boat back on the next tide.

Yeah. And what if he *didn't* go back there?

Then he's an idiot. This is a dangerous coast and—far as I could tell—he's no sailor. But even if he *has* drowned himself, if Margaret doesn't see us in a day or two she'll start to wonder.

Will she? Did you tell her how long you were planning to stay?

Not exactly. I said I'd see how you were doing—what you wanted to do.

When Margaret brought me over she came up here with me, checked things out for me—looked in the cupboards, says Bonnie. There's food here for months. Water as long as it rains occasionally, which—in case you hadn't noticed—it does here this time of year.

If she doesn't see us soon she'll wonder. She'll come by.

Maybe. She doesn't like it here. Why don't you make lunch, Larry? I'm going to lie down.

Sometime toward mid-afternoon the fog opens up a bit, the sun trying to burn through. Margaret doesn't return. I cook brown rice and lentils on the box stove—burn myself. Food for months—if you don't mind rice and beans and porridge with powdered milk. I notice Homer's casting rod hanging on the rock wall. Wonder if I could catch anything off the point? I'd probably make one cast into the wind and end up with a snarl the size of Vancouver Island. Homer never made a fisherman out of me. I was doing okay till the first time I actually caught one and he made me kill it and clean it.

I find a tin of curry powder. No label on it, but a sniff tells. No labels on *anything*, as a matter of fact. I start poking around. A biscuit tin full of garden seeds—carefully stored in envelopes— unlabeled. Bonnie's right; it *is* weird. Not only are all his precious books gone—the shelves which used to be lined with them standing empty except for a few tools and shells and bits of driftwood—it's like he's actually attempted to eliminate the written word from his surroundings completely.

Bonnie's watching me from the bed. It's creepy, she says. You can see why I just can't believe it—that whole story about his other son, with a name that's just a letter and he can't read or write. It all just sounds too much like a figment of somebody's imagination, if you ask me.

Whose imagination? Mine? I say. I don't know if Homer is alive or dead, Bonnie—I don't know what to believe anymore. But Y exists—I met him, and I do believe he is Homer's son. And my brother.

Come on, Larry. You can come clean with *me*. Where did

145

you *really* go with that lawyer? Some sleazy hotel in Langford? But hiring that creep detective to tell tales on yourself—that was a bit much, don't you think? And then bringing him here—leaving him alone with the boat. All a little too convenient, don't you think?

Convenient for who?

For *whom*, Larry. You'll have your mother turning in *her* grave, too—and she's not even dead yet, either. Both *my* parents are dead, you know.

I know.

No, I mean *really*. I always *said* they were dead because as far as *they* were concerned *I* was dead. Vice versa is fair play, isn't it? You knew that, didn't you? But now they *are* both dead—for real. Let's not lie to each other anymore, okay, Larry? My father died four years ago. My mother died last March. I never said anything. I saw the obituaries. For years—whenever I went to the library— I always checked the obituaries in the Moose Jaw *Times-Herald*. I bet you didn't know that, did you? If it had been my mother who died first, maybe I could have told you, but I *couldn't* tell you because I knew you wouldn't be able to leave it alone—just like *this* whole damn business. And then when *she* died last March— I guess I didn't see the point.

I'm sorry, Bonnie. And I *do* believe you. About Homer.

No, you don't. If you believed me you'd be doing something.

What, for Christ's sake?

I don't know. Neither do you. That's the trouble. Your lentils are burning.

Bonnie won't eat my burnt lentils, though I put in enough curry to mask the black taste. She eats brown rice. Day closes down early. Once I hear a motor, but it's only an airplane.

146

The tide comes and goes. In the last of the daylight I walk out to the point, to the place where Katherine found Homer. I wonder what it is Bonnie won't tell me? I know what I haven't told her.

A gull screams near the top of the blasted pine. The swell is low and steady and shatters to a slushy rumble on the broken rock.

I cannot believe. I cannot.

If my father is alive then who died here? The stranger—the man Margaret spoke of—obviously. A big white man with a beard, she said. But what about the dental records, then? And if Homer *were* alive, here, somehow, then *where*? There's hardly cover to hide a squirrel on this bony rock. Bonnie dreamt it—whatever she saw. Or she's making it up. She's lied to me before. Her parents alive all these years? Maybe I knew, at least suspected—she kept her past dark and I learned not to pry. But everything is different now. Something else has come between us.

When I get back up to the shack she is in bed. I don't light the lamps.

As the dark tightens and the tide comes up and the wind builds and the rock itself seems to shudder under the weight of the night—I consider some other questions. Was *I* dreaming, that night in that over-heated hotel room, when I thought I read things Homer—alive *or* dead—had no way of imagining? Did I *really* steal the final page and hide it inside that bathroom wall? Who *was* the mysterious bearded stranger Margaret spoke of? Did Homer actually have a brother we never knew about, *either*? Did *he* murder my father—forcing the whiskey down his throat—then leaving the bottle beside his body? Was Art Humble right all along?

147

Homer's bed is narrow. Exhausted and alone as I am, I can't get past the anger Bonnie wraps around herself like a feather tick. I doze in Homer's big chair, with Bonnie's bear in my arms. Once I wake to a sudden clatter and peer through the dark—fully expecting to see my father alive at his desk, pounding the keys of his old Olivetti—but it is only a smattering of hail on the roof.

Dental records could be faked, couldn't they? Anything can be faked, can't it?

I suppose so, I say. But why?

To cover up the murder, of course.

Then who *is* the victim?

Margaret said something about some guy who came here last spring. A big guy with a beard—claimed he was Homer's brother. He left his motorcycle at her place. She said he didn't stay long, but maybe he came back later in the summer and—

Wait—a motorcycle? Margaret told you he came on a motorcycle?

That's what she said.

Leo!

Who?

Leo Knotts. Zanzu's boyfriend—the one she told Y was his father. Of course! How could I be so stupid? Leo *knew* about Homer—he caught that twit Humble snooping, squeezed him till he talked. He must have come out here to settle things with Homer. Looks like he did.

Maybe Homer settled things with *him*.

Sure. Homer killed him—then knocked all his teeth out—then pulled all his own teeth and shoved them into Leo's jaw.

Fuck you, Larry. Dental records can be faked. *Anything* can be faked. I used to believe *you* really loved me.

148

Daylight is brief and obscured by the constant rain. We light the lamps in the morning and burn them till we sleep at night. Homer has half a drum of kerosene in the lean-to shed, but we are going through his firewood—fast. There's no gas for the chain-saw, but I find a flat file and start to sharpen the old Swede-saw which hangs just inside the front door. Bonnie watches me for a while, then takes the file away from me and touches up each tooth. Bloody machinist.

There are plenty of logs washed up on the rocks. We drag a couple of lengths of cedar well above high tide line, lean one across the other and set to work. In spite of our difference in size we find an easy rhythm on the saw. Inside the wood is dry and sweet.

It seems forever since I stood ankle deep in cedar shavings in my basement shop, building a box for Homer's bones. The smell is the same but the world is different.

Rain down my neck.

The rain lifts sometimes—just before sunset—and we get a sudden unexpected uncalled-for blast of dying sun, before night closes down—hard and wet. Once or twice we think we hear a boat motor, through some hole in the constant howl and whine of the wind and the grinding crash of the sea. But the tides are extreme—these waters treacherous at this time of year. Margaret does not return and no one else ventures within hailing distance of this rocky shore. We take turns in the bed, at first, but as the storms settle in and the winds pick up—testing the timbers of this makeshift shelter—we spend more time in bed, some of it together.

At some point I can't stand it—I put my arm around her. We are both fully clothed, for the bedclothes—like everything else in this world—tend to dampness. I move close to her, folding my body against hers and she doesn't move away from my warmth. My whole body aches with the sudden closeness of her. Feel it in my teeth and my knees. Between us we create an island of warmth and safety, but a part of me wants more, and when she feels that part she moves away, just a little. The cold rushes in. Rain lashes the roof.

And then the wind *really* whips in off the ocean; the waves crash on the rocks like all the bad stuff in the world battering down the back door, and Bonnie turns to me again and wraps her arms and legs tight around me, but she still turns her face away from my kiss.

When dreams come for us, we follow. There are other women in my dreams. Olivia always, but others as well—Sylvie in sackcloth and Katherine and Kate in leather—Zanzu nude and toothless—my sister dressed to kill—my mother in beads and hippie skirts. And me, punch drunk and stupid, wandering the twisted corridors, my prick in my hand.

Whatever Bonnie dreams she doesn't say.

I only came to visit Homer a couple of times after he moved out here for good. Bonnie came with me the last time, the summer after Adam went to live on the mainland. We'd taken a camping trip up-island, decided to spend our last day here at Bone Island. Bonnie was quite taken with the place, though the day turned grey and cold and Homer seemed distracted—almost annoyed by our intrusion. He fed us and questioned us for news, but seemed uninterested in our answers and shrugged off questions about his own health and his life here on this lonely rock. He said nothing about working on another book.

The first time I *ever* came here—over ten years ago—Homer brought me up to help him with some repairs and maintenance. We brought my tools and a generator and two bottles of whiskey and a couple of flats of beer. I did most of the work and Homer did most of the drinking, but we helped each other to the best of our abilities. I don't remember much of *that* weekend, but looking around I can still see—here and there—the mark of my tipsy hammer.

What were they really like—your parents? I ask Bonnie.

You are trying to change the subject, she says—though we've hardly spoken for days.

Sorry, I say.

Have you ever wondered, she says, why we have no friends?

We have friends, I say, though *she* is the one changing the subject.

Who? she says.

I think of some names but I don't say them. She's right. They are neighbors, co-workers, people we would stop and speak to in the street, maybe even invite to a party. But *friends?* Who among them would I—did I?—call on in an hour of need?

Okay, I say. Maybe you are right. I think it's because we always thought we could be enough for each other.

I know, she says. Kind of sick, isn't it?

Personally, I think it's kind of romantic, but I can see her point so I don't say anything.

There was another girl in Moose Jaw who looked a lot like

me, says Bonnie. She wasn't a local—she came from back east—but she was short and she had crazy hair just like mine. She was a hooker. My mother spotted her on a street corner. She went home and got my grandfather—the retired chief of police—and my father—the junior high school principal—and she made them drive downtown in my grandfather's van, and kidnap her and bring her home. I was twenty-four. I hadn't lived at home since I was eighteen. I'd finished my degree and I was working in the public library—but my parents didn't use the public library, so I guess they didn't know that.

My father actually grabbed the girl, and he knew as soon as he got her in the van that she wasn't me. But he was too busy trying to keep her from scratching his eyes out to explain that to my grandfather. One of the other girls on the street had the sense to get the licence number. There was a scandal—my father lost his job. I tried to call and talk to him, but my mother wouldn't let me. She never forgave me. It was like I'd planned the whole thing just to humiliate her.

I laugh. I can't help it. Bonnie doesn't laugh.

I had friends in Moose Jaw, she says.

One morning I notice a sheet of paper rolled into Homer's old Olivetti, bend over to read a single line—Anything can be faked, Larry.

Did you type this? I demand.

Type what?

I pull the page out of the typewriter and hand it to her. She reads it with no visible change of expression, hands it back to me.

No, she says, but I can tell she doesn't expect me to believe her.

152

Nothing to read. Just for a few moments to silence my own stupid thoughts. Increasingly I feel the burden of my life as somehow separate from me—a great bundle of cares, worries, troubles, confusions, which I can't do anything about and which—really— touch me not at all.

Nothing to read—nothing to talk about. All the stuff we don't say because it probably really *is* better left unsaid. Just the whine of the wind, the constant grumble of the sea.

I know the world is full of people unhappier than this. People in real pain, fearing worse pain—nothing to read—nothing to eat—nothing to believe. I could sit here and suffer for them all. Sometimes I feel I do. But isn't it better if I can let them all suffer for me?

It's okay—it's over. (Isn't it?) Y has the book and the lawyer—for better and worse. Leo Knotts has gone back to his dogs and his bagpipes and his trap-line near Wolf Lake—maybe he *did* come to see Homer, but he was gone long before Homer died, and even if he *did* come back—even if Art Humble *was* right and Homer *was* murdered—how could we ever prove anything, now?

Over. Homer is dead. Bonnie will come around, will get over these crazy scary dreams, will hold me and talk to me again— won't she? Unless, unless… Y has the book, almost. Bonnie's right, Larry, if only once in your life you could give it up—not holding anything back—there might be a chance for us…

The wind abates a little but the rain is incessant. It is nothing—it matters nothing now. Unless…The rain is relentless, drowning thought.

I remember sitting here with Homer—the last time I came alone—waiting out the rain, playing chess. We didn't talk much. He told fish stories. The big ones that got away. I talked a bit about work, and Adam and Bonnie. A space beside the chess-board on the table where the bottle wasn't. We tried to fill it with the teapot. I used to beat him, sometimes, when he was still drinking. Never since he got sober.

Bonnie hates chess. Homer's set sits open on the bookless shelves, set up to an end-game position, but an impossible one— a double checkmate. Everybody loses.

I find scissors and cut some of Homer's typing paper into pieces the size and shape of playing cards. Bonnie gives me a funny look but she gets her watercolours out of her pack and colours in the pips and faces I draw. We play go-fish. Bonnie wins every hand. This rain is not the same rain that has drowned out all our lives, but it is much the same—even if every drop is unique. Rice and beans bubble on the stove.

Go fish, says Bonnie.

Sometimes, late afternoon, the rain breaks, a hole opens in the storm, the sudden quiet overwhelms us. A bright place in the heavy-bottomed cloud where the sun might be.

Go fish, I say.

Homer's casting rod is long and perfectly balanced and his line is baited with a fluorescent green lure—a baby squid on acid, maybe. I guess it is supposed to annoy the fish—it certainly does-n't look good to eat.

I'm not much good with these, I say.

Here, says Bonnie, let me try, and she takes the rod. It is much too long for her but she leans back with both hands and lets fly far out across the rolling swell. She thumbs the reel with a machinist's precision—not a hint of backlash.

My dad used to take me fishing up north, she says. I caught a fifteen-pound jackfish when I was nine. Shit, I think I'm snagged—

A beautiful silver-sided salmon explodes out of the swell with the green lure glowing in the corner of its mouth. Bonnie lets out a cowgirl whoop and leans back on the rod. She plays the fish hard, grinning like a nine-year-old.

Homer always promised he'd take me salmon fishing some-day, she says, as she finally guides the tired fish between two rocks, where I manage—on the third try—to grab it by the tail and haul it up the shore. Bonnie kills it quickly—a single sharp blow on the head with a fist-sized stone.

You got your knife?

I hand her my Swiss Army knife and she slits the quivering coho and scrapes its entrails out onto the rocks. She rinses the gutted fish and the knife in a tide-pool—sticks the knife in her pocket—carries the salmon up to the shack. I bring Homer's rod. There's foil in a drawer, so we stuff the fish with rice and wrap it and bake it right inside the firebox.

While we are waiting we play crazy eights. Dark slides in and the rain resumes, but gentle, almost soothing…Bonnie still wins every hand.

Later, in bed, we bundle. Bonnie talks about fishing at Lac La Ronge with her father, about going out with him in the canoe at night with a flashlight to watch the bullfrogs sing, about seeing the northern lights so bright and crazy—eating up the whole sky with colour—that she fell over backwards in the canoe and just lay there watching.

When I was eleven I got my period, she says. My mother

decided no more fishing trips. Not appropriate for a *young woman.*

I wake at first light. The rain has stopped. The fire is out and the place is cold and the chimney stinks of creosote and charred fish bones. I cling closer to Bonnie's warm solid breathing and she snuggles closer too. I venture a gentle kiss on her lips and she wrinkles her nose and turns her face away, without opening her eyes.

I sigh and start to roll away from her, but she grabs me by the belt loop and pulls me back against her, now, and she kisses me—her breath warm and sour on my face.

I dreamt I caught a big fish, she says, unzipping my pants.

That wasn't a dream, I say.

No, she says, this was a *really* big fish.

Her hand in my pants now, her chilly fingers swarming over me. I am half-blind and breathless with a sudden rush of yearning—my toes almost cramp with the flex of it. Bonnie has that same delighted nine-year-old look on her face.

Somehow a ray of sunshine penetrates the salt-grimed glass. I thumb Bonnie's buttons, my heart pounding furiously in the hollow of my chest. I push her legs apart with my knee, press hard into her heat. I am hard as a burl under her teasing fingers and feeling for the snap of her jeans when we both hear it—the looming purr of Margaret's outboard.

Margaret sits down on a big rock beside her boat, fills her insulated mug from a steaming thermos. Bonnie and I—our pants fastened—crowd into the doorway and watch Adam and Katherine pick their way up the hill. Clouds cover the sun, but the air is clear, no fog at all—you can almost see a real horizon. The sea strangely quiet, slack tide.

What happened to Homer's boat? Katherine asks, when she is close enough to speak without raising her voice.

Arthur Humble stole it, I say.

Who?

Art Hamilton's cousin—Art, I say. She gives me a weird look.

Guess it's a good thing we decided to drop by.

Adam hugs Bonnie, then me. Leila left Duncan, he says. She's staying at our house on Speed Avenue. Liz keeps calling from New York. She says she has to talk to you—it's urgent, but she wouldn't tell me what it was all about. I figured I should try and get in touch. Oh, and Sylvie's pregnant. How are you guys doing?

I look at Bonnie.

We're fine, I say. Bonnie giggles.

We tidy up a little and go. Crowding into Margaret's boat, speaking little as she eases between the sheltering rocks and angles into

157

the swell. Katherine points out the spot where she found the body. She doesn't have to speak. *Nothing but grief,* I told him, says Margaret.

Bonnie, alone in the bows, keeps looking back, as if she expects to see Homer—peeking out from behind a rock or something. She does that till we clear the next headland, out of sight of Bone Island. I look back a couple of times myself.

Margaret's grandsons have already got Art Humble's Volaré out of the woods and up on blocks and one of them is smoking and humming to himself underneath it. Katherine's white Toyota is pulled in beside my truck.

I tried giving Adam directions when he called, she says, but then he said something about hitchhiking and I thought I'd better step in. I wanted to come up and see Margaret, anyway. I was in pretty rough shape last time I was here—I'm not sure I'd have made it without her.

We warm our hands on a mug of tea. Adam wants to catch a ferry; he's got classes in the morning. I slip Margaret a couple more of Homer's old fifties. The cloud cover has closed tight now, no sign of the sun. Bonnie hugs Margaret and Katherine and gets into the truck. Adam thanks Katherine—shakes her hand—gets in beside Bonnie.

I'm going to stay and have another cup of tea with Margaret, says Katherine. Watch those logging trucks, Larry.

Margaret shakes my hand but Katherine refuses my hand— hugs me hard. Call me, Larry. I think it's time you came clean with me, she says.

I'll call you.

A man—alone in his pickup—though the two people he loves the most in the world ride beside him.

Sylvie's decided to keep the baby, says Adam. It's not due till after my finals—thank God. If she can't find another job right away, she might move over—if we can find a place. Her mother is giving her grief. Me—I'm pretty freaked. I know I want to be with her. She's not sure.

Bonnie reaches for his hand, holds it between hers, in her lap. I try to remember how I felt when Bonnie told me *she* was pregnant. I wasn't much older than Adam—just a kid, too—and Bonnie wasn't sure, either. Now we are going to be grandparents. Just like that. So how come I feel so all alone?

It starts to rain, like it had never stopped. The road disappears in a wash of falling sky. Hands welded to the steering wheel. I'm glad I finally got to see Bone Island, says Adam. I always meant to go visit Homer out there. I wish I had.

At the ferry terminal we all get out. I give Adam a hug—thinking how skinny he is but how much he reminds me of Homer. It's not till I'm about to get back in the truck that I realize Bonnie has her pack on and she's not getting back in. I'm sorry, Larry, she says. I'll call you.

What?

It's *your* shit, Larry. I've had it up to here.

I'll come with you, then.

You can't. They'll tow your truck if you leave it here. Go make up with your sister, Larry. Go call your mother. Go see Sylvie and tell her congratulations from me, too. I'll be there when the baby comes—I promise. I love you the whole way, too, Larry, but some things we just can't do for each other. Take care of yourself.

159

She kisses me—the whole way—once, leaves me breathless. Alone.

A man—alone in his pickup—watching the ferry pull away.

A man, alone in his truck on a dead end street. Parked in front of his own home—alone. It is dark by the time I make Speed Avenue, and it is still raining. The lights are on in the front room, but the blinds are still up—Sylvie and Leila are on the sofa. Leila is concentrating on something she is doing with her hands, then she lifts them enough that I can see she is knitting. I've never seen my sister knit before. I know our mother never taught her. Concentrating like that she looks a little like Homer and a lot like Adam. Which probably means she looks a lot like me.

I turn the truck off but I don't get out. I sit and watch them. Leila talks—Sylvie listens, laughs. I shut my eyes and try to picture the tiny fetus inside her, jiggling in the sac of her laughter. Grampa Larry. Christ, I haven't even begun to get over not being young anymore.

Leila puts her knitting down and gets up to close the blind. She looks right at me but gives no sign that she sees me. Without waiting for her to finish lowering the blind, I start the truck and drive away. Don't know where I'm going, but for a start I cruise by the warehouse site. They've finished the flashing on the parapets. The hoarding is locked and I can tell from my truck it's a new padlock. My sign is gone and a new one—carefully hand-lettered—reads:

T. Lander Construction
General Contractor

So—Tim has taken over the job. Good for him. Wonder

160

how he and Duncan are getting along? I don't stop. Drive downtown, cruise by the bookstore, over the blue bridge, find myself parked at another curb—this one in Vic West—in front of the little brown house where Katherine and Kate live.

Time to come clean, Larry? I don't know. I'm disappointed to find Katherine's Toyota already in the driveway. I was hoping she wouldn't be home yet, that Kate would open the door in surprise but invite me in, that we would wait together, with something warm to drink—that Kate's casual hearty cynicism would take the edge off my shame and my confusion, ease me into a confessional space.

Again I sit in my truck, unable to get out. The house is a little shit-brown one-bedroom bungalow and only one light still burns—in the bedroom. No movement behind drawn curtains. Can they be in bed this early? Maybe driving on logging roads makes Katherine horny. I picture them in the rumpled bed, moist and short of breath, let the image linger till my lap starts to grow a bone. What the hell is wrong with me?

I start the truck and drive. I cruise Esquimalt—out through View Royal—concentrate on the driving, light to light, till I wind up in Langford. When my erection subsides it occurs to me I should be hungry, so I pull into the Log House Pub and eat some pub food and drink a couple of mugs of draft beer and watch part of a very boring hockey game on TV.

I break another of Homer's old fifties. Still got quite a stack. The place isn't crowded so I buy a round for the house and suddenly I have friends. I am unable to avoid drinking several more mugs of beer before I finally make it out of there and back to my truck.

I sit in the truck for a couple of minutes, trying to decide if I am too drunk to drive, then I stagger back into the pub—find the telephone and call my mother.

It is very late in New York, but she answers on the second ring.

Hi, Mom.

Larry. Where are you calling from?

The Log House Pub in Langford. Do I sound like I'm too drunk to drive?

I knew it. Adam said you'd gone to Bone Island—to find Bonnie. I knew it couldn't be you. But Walter *swore* he saw you day before yesterday on Seventh Avenue and you had your arm around some black-haired woman. I thought it must have been that lawyer.

You'd better check Walter's medication.

I knew you wouldn't come to New York and not call me. What's going on, Larry? I've been worried. I called your place and got Leila.

Yeah. That's why I'm here—not there. I've got friends here. Drunks, mostly, but beggars can't be choosers, eh? There's at least a couple of women in this pub who will probably fuck me if I buy them another drink.

You're drunk.

That's what I thought. Guess I'd better call a cab. Can I crash at your place tonight, Mom?

You said you weren't in New York.

I'm not. But I've got lots of cab fare.

Don't be silly. Listen, Larry. You'd better call your sister. I think she needs you. I've never heard her sound so—happy. I think she's having some kind of a manic spell. She may do something.

She already is. She's knitting. Baby booties, I suppose.

Baby booties?

Oops. Cat out of the bag. I guess Adam didn't tell you.

Adam? You don't mean he's knocked up that sweet child?

162

Sylvie.

She's not going to go through with it?

Apparently.

Dear God. After all the blood we spilled for the right to choose.

She's chosen, I guess.

I suppose you are right. Oh dear, what is *happening* to us? You *did* find Bonnie, didn't you? She *is* okay, isn't she?

She's fine. She sends her love.

That lie seems to go over okay, so I try another—Look, somebody wants to use the phone.

Don't hang up, Larry, she says, but I already have.

The fresh air makes me feel better. I get in my truck and drive— crank the window open. The truck responds to my touch like a living thing. I feel an unusual rapport, a fluid ambiguity that seems reassuring, almost sensual. I am quite certain I can make it without hitting anything, and even if I *do* hit anything—I can't imagine it will hurt. Everything has a soft look.

I lied to my mother. No woman in that bar would have fucked me if I bought her a brewery. I'm just a dangerous creep— drunk in his truck.

By the time I get to town, I'm weeping so hard I miss Speed Avenue. I want to make a U-turn but I spot a cop coming the other way and I try to concentrate—keep a grip—ease through the green lights. Next thing you know I'm in fucking Fairfield. Occurs to me the least I can do is stop at Leila's house and tell Duncan I'm sorry I ruined his car.

He comes to the door in his tartan pajamas, a green bottle in one hand, fuzzy slippers. He doesn't seem particularly pleased to see me. Hope I didn't get you out of bed, chief? I say, but I don't get any farther because he puts down his Perrier and punches me in the nose.

My glasses go flying. I see blood—hear the crunch of bone—feel the shock like walking into a door, the pain drilling clean through to the back of my skull. Then I taste the blood, and my mind clears. I see him—standing there, clutching his hand—all his self-righteous anger draining away, replaced in his face by a mask of indignant pain. I decide not to kill him. It would be easy. I'm not a fighter but I know that I could kill him easily, with my two hands, drunk as I am.

I pick up my glasses from the lawn. They are bent but not broken. I turn and walk back to my truck. It isn't raining hard, but it's steady and I'm getting wet—it feels good. I get out my handkerchief, dab at the blood which trickles from my nose. Doesn't feel broken, though. Must have been his knuckle I heard crack. His face is still stretched by the pain of it, but he yells at me.

Call the cops—*charge* me with assault! I don't give a fuck, Larry.

I'm glad Tim still has a job, I say. What about Sylvie?

If she gets rid of the baby she can have her job back.

You're joking.

Read my lips, Larry. Fuck you. Fuck all of you. Sylvie's a nice kid but you and your clan are going to chew her up and spit her out, just like the rest of us. Well I don't want any part of it. No Knee works for me again—not even in the womb.

Maybe I should kill him after all. Not because he's wrong but because he's right.

I get in my truck and drive.

Drive. Never felt more sober in my life.

Speed Avenue is dark—another streetlight burnt out. The house is dark. I let myself in quietly.

I can smell my sister. I find her in my bedroom—naked in my bed with a candle, a bottle of tequila and a brace of limes. When I open the door she lets out a little shriek and pulls her hand out of her crotch. She sloshes her drink trying to put it down and pull the sheet up over her breasts at the same time. I'd forgotten what nice tits she had.

I didn't think you'd be coming back tonight, she says. I saw you drive away.

I didn't plan to, I say, but I was too drunk to think of anywhere else to go.

What happened with Bonnie?

We don't have any friends. Have you noticed that?

What are you talking about?

I guess we're even, now, I say. For the time you caught me jacking off in the garage when we were thirteen.

Can't a girl scratch herself?

I can smell you from here—even with a swollen nose.

You're disgusting. What *happened* to your nose, anyway?

Your husband socked me.

What did you do to him?

Nothing. I was trying to apologize.

And he *hit* you? *Duncan*?

I think he hurt his hand. A noble gesture, though—you have to admit.

What an idiot. I'm letting him keep the business, you know. And the house.

And *you* are calling *him* an idiot?

Shut up, Larry. Listen, Larry—I don't need him. Any more than I need you.

Thanks. So can I have my bed back?

She moves over, offers me the bottle. When it is empty we hold each other and cry ourselves to sleep.

I wake from crumbling dreams in my own bed, but it is full of tangled limbs and only some of them are mine. I find a nice pair of legs and when I try a knee between them they open wide. When the rest of me tries to follow, the woman they belong to wakes with a yelp and I notice that she is my sister and roll off her.

For a long time we lie there in the semi-darkness—not speaking or touching—but each aware of the wakefulness of the other. Finally Leila breaks the silence. You're just like Homer, she says, condemning me once and for all. I say nothing, but I wonder if she is accusing me for what I almost tried. Or because I stopped.

I remember Olivia—*He tried, Larry. You didn't even try.*

I get up and go into the bathroom. The floor pitching and rolling like a ship. I lift the lid and fall on my knees and puke into the bowl. It is an easy, fiery release. Bits of all the crap I ate at the pub—chicken wings and nachos and sausage rolls and pretzels—all swimming in beer and bile and tequila.

I flush a couple of times, hug the bowl for a while, feeling a whole lot better, thanks. Eventually, I feel well enough to let go of the bowl and slither out of my clothes and stand under the shower. The beer was fine—you were doing okay with the beer, Larry. The tequila—*that* was a mistake. What were you thinking, mixing the grain and the goddamn *cactus*, Larry? The hot water beats a fabulous tattoo on my neck—I move under it, bend my knees, take it right on top of my head, let the water beat on me, drown me out—ceaseless as the rain, but hot, almost too hot to stand.

166

When the last traces of soap are down the drain, I turn off the taps and stand for a long time, listening to my body drip. Wonder if Leila is still awake in the bedroom? Got to get out of here. All my clean clothes are in the bedroom but I don't want to go back in there. My dirty clothes lie in a heap on the bathroom floor—flecked with vomit and salmon scales and stinking of sweat and tequila and fish and wood smoke. I retrieve my wallet and keys—check the pockets again and notice that my Swiss Army knife is gone. I remember Bonnie slipping it into her pocket after she cleaned that salmon. I guess I never got it back. I gather my dirty clothes in a bundle, which I hold at arm's length till I get it down to the laundry.

Maybe Adam has something that will fit me. Even though he's been living on the mainland for two years he's still got a closet full of clothes here. I've got twenty-five pounds on him, but some of his stuff might stretch.

Sylvie is asleep in Adam's bed. I sense her there and don't turn on the light. She sleeps very peacefully; in the cracked grey light from the basement window she looks very young and a little sad. I stand and look at her for a few moments, then move to the closet. By feel, I come up with a pair of stretchy red sweat-pants that are only a little short, and an over-sized green wool pullover. I guess I look like some kind of Christmas tree ornament, but I stop shivering.

The clock in the kitchen says it's nearly three. Need some air. It has stopped raining. Out on the porch the air is sharp and clear, though everything still glistens from the recent drench. I walk past my truck—don't even look at it. I'm twice as sober now as I was before (or leastwise only half as drunk?) but I've dodged enough lead already tonight. Walk it off, Larry. You never were a

167

good boozer, face it. Should've danced with the drug that got you here. But Jimmy, the herbalist down the street, is fast asleep like everybody else in the world. I walk downtown instead.

As I walk, a plan comes to me. Tim lives in a float-house at Fisherman's Wharf—maybe I can crash the rest of the night there. Tim won't be thrilled to be wakened so early, but by the time I walk there it will be later and he probably won't punch me. His girlfriend might.

I stroll. The streets are empty, clean, glittering; a few yellow and blue cabs swish around; a drunk crosses the street when he sees me coming. Maybe it's the clothes. A woman standing on a street corner asks me for a light. She's young, but not as young as she's trying to look; she's got nervous friendless eyes; her pale skin is made to look almost deathly by the brutal colours of her make-up. She's dressed like a whore.

I apologize, feeling pockets.

Never mind, she says. Want to go somewhere?

I stop and look at her. You'd really do it with somebody who dressed like this? I say.

If we went somewhere you could get undressed, she says.

I appreciate the offer, I say. Really—I do, but I'm only having a crisis or something. I love my wife—but she's left me. She's in Moose Jaw, with her friends. Listen—have one of these. I dig out my wallet, offer her one of Homer's fifties.

Hey, she says, not here in the street—but she takes the bill, makes it disappear.

That belonged to my father, I say. He's dead. Big guy—grey beard—very well hung. He'd want you to have it.

You're weird, she says.

Down around the inner harbour, two guys start following me. I pick up the pace a little, but they keep gaining. Must be my Christmas get-up—they've picked me out as a queer—going to get my head broken. I keep walking, steady—looking left and right for a weapon. They are almost up to me when I catch the glint of an empty wine bottle rolled up against the curb.

I don't even think. Just bend over, grab the bottle by the neck and smack it against the curb, step away from them into the street, brandishing the jagged bottleneck. They face me for a moment—big guy and little guy—faces broken open with surprise, and then I am flooded with headlights as a patrol car rounds the corner.

The two guys make a wide circle around me—no more eye contact—keep walking. The cop car stops in the middle of the street, holding me frozen in headlights like a pit-lamped deer. The cop waits till the two guys are around the corner, then gets slowly out of his car. There is a litter barrel a few feet away—I toss the broken bottle in. The cop is tall and blond and young. He chews gum while he talks.

Kind of nervous tonight? he says.

No problem, officer. Just a little clumsy. Saw that empty bottle—thought I'd just toss it in the can—just gave it a little bump. I'll just clean up the—

You got some I.D.?

Sure.

I dig out my wallet. Snap open the card holder. There's my library card, and an expired free pass to the Crystal Pool, and a two year old receipt from Slegg Lumber. The rest of the plastic flaps are empty. No driver's licence—no credit cards—no Carecard. No journeyman ticket, no birth certificate, no citizenship card.

It's gone, I say, stupidly.

What's gone?

Everything—all my I.D.

I remember the prostitute I was talking to—could she—somehow—but when I spread the billfold, the rest of Homer's fifties are still there. The cop's eyes narrow.

You got no I.D.?

I've been robbed. Look—all they left was my library card. I extract the blue card and try to hand it to him. It has my signature and a bar code—no personal information. He ignores it.

Took your I.D. and left all that cash? One for the books, he says.

I have to report this. They got my credit cards.

That's a lot of cash, he says.

My—my father gave that to me. Left it to me. He's dead.

I see. No wonder you were a little nervous, carrying that much cash—this time of night.

I see what you mean. Actually, I wasn't thinking about the money. They were gay-bashers, those guys. They were ready to jump me. *They're* the ones you should be talking to.

I'm talking to you. I think maybe you'd better come along up to the station so we can get to the bottom of this.

Yes. I mean no. I mean—can't I just tell *you*, then you can call it in? You're a cop, aren't you?

Get in the car.

He's a cop, all right. It is warm and dry in the back of the patrol car, but I can't stop shivering.

At the police station I have to tell it all to another cop—also young, tall, blond—she might be his sister. She asks me questions, types my answers into her computer. She makes me count out the money from my wallet—twelve hundred and sixty-two dollars and change. She makes me put Homer's twenty-four remaining fifties in an envelope, gives me a receipt.

Does this mean I'm being arrested for something?

Why? Have you done something?

I just wondered why you are taking my money?

I gave you a receipt. Wait over there.

I wait. All sorts of things going through my head. Was that prostitute really an undercover cop? When was the last time I used any of my missing cards? Been paying cash for everything since Olivia gave me that stack of fifties. Who's had access to my wallet, then? Bonnie? Art Humble maybe—that night we slept at Margaret's? But why would *he* take my I.D.? Why would *anybody*?

Finally another cop comes and takes me into an office. The cop in the office wears a suit and isn't young, tall *or* blond. Homer's money is spread out on the table in front of him.

Sit down, please.

I sit down.

Want to tell me where you got this money?

From my father. From his lawyer, actually. My father's dead. Is there something wrong with it? I know it's *old*. Is it counterfeit or something?

Tell me about your father.

His name was Homer Knee. He was a writer. He lived the last few years on a little island off the coast—Bone Island. He was found dead there around the end of October, died of exposure. I've got no idea where *he* got the money. His lawyer's name is Olivia Astrakhan. She's out of town right now.

Inconvenient. I know the name. Handles a lot of drug cases, doesn't she?

I don't know.

Your father involved with drugs?

Homer? No. He used to drink a lot of Irish whiskey—but

he'd been sober for five years.

You say he was a writer? Don't think I know the name.

He wasn't well known. He used to run a book store, here in town.

What about you, Larry? That's your name, Larry? *You* into drugs?

Just this evening I made the mistake of drinking tequila on top of dark draft beer.

He smiles for the first time, gets up from the desk, puts his hands in his pockets. I get the feeling he would like to turn away and stand and look out the window—only the office doesn't have any windows. Maybe he used to have an office with a window. He stands and looks at me, instead.

What's all this shit about drugs? I say. Somebody lifted my I.D. and my credit cards out of my wallet. They could be out there charging stuff and committing crimes of fraud right now—while we sit here chatting about my father's literary career and *my* recreational tastes.

He keeps looking at me. We traced the money, he says. We knew it had to be funny—that many out-dated fifties. It took a while because it *was* old. Turns out that money was part of a pay-off in a big drug sting—years ago—a big RCMP operation out of Nanaimo. Somebody screwed up—the bad guys got away, with the money. None of it ever turned up. Till now.

All they found was their shoes? I say.

Eventually I tell him most of it. I leave out a few details, of course—the mushrooms at Homer's funeral—the joint passed at the urinal—the page hidden in the wall. The ghost Bonnie saw. But I *do* suggest murder, even name Leo Knotts as a likely suspect, well aware that I am just smoke-screening—me with my library card and my bloody nose and my mismatched ill-fitting clothes and my funny money and even funnier story. I see, as I talk, that I am walking a fine line between ending up in a cell here or under observation in a psych ward at the Eric Martin Pavilion. I try to round up my stampeding narrative—he paces behind his chair, letting me hang myself, not believing a word. When I run down he leaves me to think it over, but he's back ten minutes later, his cynical frown replaced by a smug sneer.

Why don't we go back to the beginning, Larry? That *is* your name?

Larry Knee, I say. As in kneecap.

Well, we have a little problem, Larry. See, I just called your home phone number and talked to your sister. She insists you are in New York City.

It is Sylvie who rescues me. The detective and I are still there in that windowless office—the tainted money still spread like a stain on the desk. I sit, my bones turning to cement, my truths sounding more like lies by the minute—even to me. He continues to pace, hands still in his pockets, but now he is doing more of the talking, suggesting alternative scenarios, more plausible ones, I have to admit, ugly little scenarios involving an unidentified man with a pocket full of dirty fifties and a stolen library card, who doesn't want to tell police his real name—who seems to think that by spinning a web of impossible lies he will convince them that he is too eccentric to be dangerous.

His phone rings. He picks it up, frowns, grunts.

Send her in, he says, puts the phone down. To me he says, Your daughter is here to identify you. Funny, I don't think you mentioned you had a daughter?

Before I can figure out what the hell he's talking about,

173

Sylvie is there in the doorway, wearing baggy flannel pants and Adam's tree-planting jacket, her hair wildly unbrushed. She looks like she just tumbled out of bed. Hi, Larry, she says—I heard Leila telling someone on the phone that you were in New York but I saw your truck out front so I knew you weren't. She told me it was the police so I thought you might be in trouble. I told them I was your daughter because I was afraid they might not let me in if I told them I was just your son's girlfriend. I mean—me and Adam aren't even living together yet—even if we *are* pregnant. I'm just sleeping in his room for a while—my mother threw me out—which is why I was there and heard Leila on the phone in the first place—so I hope it was okay?

The detective stares at her. She smiles at him. He turns away, remembers there's no window, shrugs, looks at his watch, sits down.

This is giving me a headache, he says. Get out of here—both of you. Don't leave town without telling us, Larry. It might give somebody the wrong idea.

What about the money? I say.

We'll be holding on to the money—at least till we get to the bottom of this. Just tell me one more thing, Larry—why would your sister lie to us?

My sister is a pathological liar, I say. Didn't I mention that? It runs in the family.

Outside the streets are still damp but the sky is clear, and long red rays of sunshine flash off the glass of the downtown towers. My truck is there, parked in the tow-away zone in front of the station.

I remembered you always keep that extra key under your toolbox, says Sylvie.

You'd better drive, I say. Somebody ripped off my licence.

Who?

I've got an idea about that, but it's too crazy.

She gets into the driver's seat. I'm starving, she says. You want to go have breakfast somewhere?

We go to the Red Mango, sit by the window. I get coffee—Sylvie has mint tea.

No more drugs till I'm done nursing, she says.

Good for you, I say.

I hope you didn't mind me saying I was your daughter, Larry?

Hey. I like it a lot better than my sister denying I'm her brother. But maybe I'm better off with a daughter like you than a sister like her.

Hey, don't say that, Larry. Leila's cool—she's just awful wound up in herself these days. She's a lot like you, you know. She's been really nice to me, since my mom threw me out and

175

Duncan fired me. My mother is the bitch-queen of the universe. She wanted me to get an abortion. When I said no—she threw me out. Isn't that sick?

You must really want this baby.

I think I do, Larry. I mean, I wasn't sure, because I really love Adam, but he's so—wound up in himself, too, I guess... Do you think it's unfair of me?

I think you've got a lot of guts. Duncan laid the same trip on you, too, I take it?

Hunh?

Fired you because you wouldn't get an abortion.

Who told you that?

He did.

He's so full of shit! He didn't even know I was pregnant when he fired me. He fired me because I laughed at what you did to his car.

I guess Tim didn't laugh.

Tim thought it was a waste of good concrete.

He was right, I say. We eat toasted bagels with cream cheese and crab-apple jelly. I drink more coffee—the sun comes up like it was never gone—the day shines—traffic on Quadra builds to a lurching crawl. I tell Sylvie about Bone Island, about the smuggler's tainted money, about Leo Knotts and even about Bonnie's mysterious visitation. Sylvie stirs honey into her tea.

I wish I could've known Homer better, she says. He seemed so kind. Sounds like he was a bit of a control freak, though.

Yeah, you could say that.

Leila sure hates him. She says he was a tyrant. Is Adam something like him?

A tyrant? Adam?

No, not a tyrant. But a bit of a control freak, maybe?

A kind-hearted control freak? Maybe. Adam reminds me of

176

Homer sometimes—something about the eyes. But I think he's more grounded. Bonnie grounds all of us.

Except maybe herself?

Apparently.

Poor Larry. You look like shit.

Thanks.

So what was Homer like? Was he a good dad?

Christ. Who knows how to be a good parent?

You and Bonnie did pretty good, I think.

Thanks. But maybe we just got lucky. Homer tried—when he wasn't drinking. When he was drinking he either forgot to try or he tried too hard. He and Leila were always at each other over something. He and Liz never really fought much—they just spent less and less time together. By the time they finally split it seemed like it had always been inevitable. Nobody made a big deal out of it. It was part of the breakdown of everything. Revolution was in the air.

Did your mom know he had this other kid?

No. But she knew he'd had more than one fling. And then she went and got involved with someone who actually cared what she thought and felt about things.

Walter?

Yes. Homer had always been too busy thinking and feeling things himself to pay much attention to her thoughts and feelings.

Sylvie spreads jelly on a corner of bagel. What *did* he think and feel? she says. What did he *love*?

What?

Homer—what did he love?

Let's see—good malt whiskey. Books—thick novels especially—Henry James, Henry Miller, Dostoevski... Fishing—trout, salmon—steelhead. He loved music. Mozart—but also blues and rock and roll—Jimi Hendrix.

MacPherson's Lament, she says.

Yes—and singing, of course. He had a beautiful baritone voice, as you remember. That was beautiful—what you said at the memorial.

Thanks. So what did he hate?

Where to begin? He hated snobs. He hated people who whistled. He hated when my sister sang off-key. He hated Republicans and Nazis and John Birchers and Senator Joe MacCarthy. He hated bigots and prudes and fundamentalists. He hated things you couldn't fix with a socket set and a multi-driver. He hated neckties.

Somebody told me that men who hate ties were probably hanged in a previous life, she says, licking jelly off her fingers.

Very likely, I say. Let's see—Homer hated onions and leeks and rutabagas and he hated digging and marching and officers and hospitals—all of which he'd had his fill of during the war. He wasn't particularly fond of physical labour of any kind—though he was very strong, and reasonably good with his hands. He hated editors and agents and publishers and literary types of every stripe. Shall I go on?

Wow. Maybe he really *was* one of those misanthropists. It's funny—he just seemed so peaceful and kind of Zen, that only time I met him—singing on the ladder…

Homer hated broadly but maybe not too deeply, I say. Mostly he was just a kind control freak, like you said. A benevolent tyrant, maybe. I guess my sister has her own opinion.

I wonder why he doesn't want to rest in peace, she says.

Apparently he's not finished with us yet.

That's creepy. Are you going to finish that?

Go ahead.

Thanks. I don't seem to have morning sickness or anything,

but I sure am hungry…I didn't get pregnant on purpose, okay? But I *did* kind of let it happen. Adam always used a condom, but this time there was something wrong with it, I guess. It kind of broke. I told him I was going to go get the morning-after pill— but then I didn't do it. I can't blame him for being pissed off at me.

He'll get over it.

I hope so. I look at my mother and some of what's been going on in *your* family and I wonder if *anybody* ever really gets over *anything*.

I drink more coffee. Sylvie has taken my truck, gone back to Speed Avenue to get me some clothes, my toothbrush. I'm still not ready to face Leila again. Don't know what I *am* ready to do, but I guess I'll try Adam in Vancouver for a start—maybe catch up with Bonnie. If she's gone on to Moose Jaw, I'll follow her there. Fuck this shit. Leave it and follow her anywhere. My identity is gone, apparently, melting away from me. Why not start a new life, then? A good carpenter can make a living anywhere, can't he? We'll settle in Moose Jaw, maybe—her friends and family will get to know me, to like me—maybe in the end they'll convince her of what I always thought she always knew…

Sylvie is gone a long time. If I drink any more coffee, I'll start to sizzle. I turn my cup over and use the washroom. When I come out she is back, my backpack full of clothes in one hand, a thick white envelope in the other. I almost forgot, she says. This came while you were gone.

I take the envelope and I know, as soon a I feel it, what is inside. No return address—but the postmark is New York City.

My name and address written large in a clean bold hand. I rip the envelope and slide my I.D. cards out on the table. They are all there—folded inside a piece of blue stationary from the Pontiac House Hotel. I read the note, then show it to Sylvie.

Dear Larry,
Sorry to be such a sneak, but there wasn't any other way. Hope you haven't missed these too much. Please believe that none of this was my idea. Kindest regards to you and Bonnie,
Olivia

I call Adam from the airport, get his machine. I picture Bonnie, sitting there in his apartment listening to my message, but if she *is* there, she doesn't pick up.

Hey, Adam—and Bonnie—if you're there. Love you both more than anything but I've got to get to the bottom of this. I'm off to New York—no idea how long I'll be gone. Maybe you're right, Bonnie—maybe Homer *is* alive. *Somebody* told Olivia Astrakhan to steal my I.D. and use it to smuggle my half-brother into the States, disguised as me. I don't know why, but it smacks of Homer to me, so if he isn't alive then he is sure as hell haunting me, and all I know is—and then the machine cuts me off with a beep, which is probably just as well because I truthfully haven't got a clue *what* I know. I hang up.

I kiss Sylvie goodbye at the security gate, go to catch my plane.

I don't have a drink on the airplane, but Walter buys very good Scotch and I accept a stiff one.

You're looking good, Larry, he says. You still look young for your age. Not quite so good-looking as that impostor I saw the other day, maybe. He had the glasses, the beard, the pony tail—and that half-perplexed, half-amused expression of yours. God knows my eyes aren't what they were—but I'd have bet my job it was you.

If you think Larry is looking good then your eyes are shot, suggests my mother. You've broken your nose, Larry.

I broke my nose playing ball when I was twelve, I say. Duncan just bent it a little.

I knew he was a hoodlum. I hope you didn't hurt him.

Just his fist.

Walter laughs.

Later, over a few more drinks, I tell them most of it. It's getting to be a story now—with each retelling it takes on its own life. I hear myself telling—embellishing a little as the Scotch takes hold—editing always, of course.

I show them the note from Olivia.

I don't get it, says Walter.

My mother snorts. She used Larry's I.D. to smuggle the bastard across the border, she says. Made him up to look like Larry—

the glasses—the pony tail. They fooled *you*—the border guards never had a chance.

But *why?* Walter still looks baffled.

Y has no identification of his own, I say. Legally he doesn't exist, or so he claims.

That's ridiculous, says Walter. And even if it *were* true—I still don't get it. The woman's a *lawyer.* She's aware of the penalties for that kind of shenanigan. What was so important about bringing him *here* that she would take that kind of risk?

The book, says my mother. It's obvious, isn't it? New York is the center of the *world* when it comes to publishing.

That might explain why she would want to bring the *book* to New York. But why the kid?

Because he comes with it, apparently. And because he *is* a kid. A young, good-looking, sexy kid. Good Lord, Walter, you used to *work* in publishing—you know what goes on.

Indeed, my dear, I don't know very much. Even if what you imply is true—I still don't see the point. It's not as if the boy had *written* the book. Larry said he couldn't even *read* it.

You know that. *I* know that. *Larry* knows that. But the people who matter in the New York publishing world don't know that—and I'll bet my bloomers Ms. Lawyer Ashcans isn't going to tell them.

That's silly. They'd never fall for it. Believe it or not—most people in publishing *do* have a brain. And even if someone *did* fall for it, the whole thing would blow up in their faces as soon as it went public. Do you think she imagines that you and Larry are going to remain silent and let them get away with it?

That's part of her plan. Nothing like a scandal to stimulate sales. She's a ruthless woman.

What do you think, Larry? Walter turns to me.

I don't know what to think. Maybe Liz is right—crazy as it sounds. But personally I don't care *what* they do with the fucking book. I want to see them. I want to ask her what she means by this note. Because I believe her. It *isn't* her idea.

After Walter goes to bed, my mother and I finish the bottle. I'm starting to feel like I'm just part of the furniture, but it's not a bad feeling.

I always liked you better than your sister, Larry. I think you should know that. She always knew.

What?

I was jealous of both of you, of course. You had each other. Whom did I have?

Homer?

Ha. I'm sorry, Larry. I'm sorry I couldn't give you the love you needed. It wouldn't have been fair to her.

I don't understand any of this. I think you're drunk.

Of course I'm drunk. So are you, for once. How'd you turn out to be such a sober soul, Larry? Spawned by a couple of old sots like me and Homer?

I've hardly been much of a sober soul *lately*, I say. But then—I seem to be losing *any* sense of identity I ever pretended to possess.

If I'd only had a year or two between you, Larry, I might have been able to handle it. I wasn't ready for twins. Neither was Homer. When Leila had her breakdown, I blamed him completely, you know. That's what really finished it for us. His affairs ticked me off but they never really mattered…I was the one who found her after she drank that stuff…

I was the one who sent her the acid, I say. Larry—the sober soul.

It wasn't *your* fault. *Or* Homer's.

Or yours, I say. You saved her life.

She *knew* I'd find her. She knew whom to punish.

Don't be stupid.

Are you and Bonnie going to be all right, Larry?

I wish I knew.

I'm glad you came. But I can't help feeling you should be with *her* right now.

Me too. I've fucked up just about everything, so far. I guess coming here was a mistake, too. What was I thinking? New York is a big place. And even if I *could* find them—I don't know…

I'll get Walter to make some calls tomorrow. He still knows people in the trade, even though he gave it up to be a saint.

He seems happy in his new life, I say.

It's incredible, isn't it? I guess there's nothing like surrounding yourself with misery to gain a sense of inner peace. What amazes me is that he still puts up with *me*.

What does he *do* down there?

Makes soup for drug addicts—hands out condoms to prostitutes—that sort of thing. I wish I'd known him years ago. I wish he could have been a father to you and Leila.

Listen, Mother—there's something I didn't mention. The manuscript that Y and Olivia have—it isn't all there.

What?

I—I stole the last page.

Whatever for?

I don't know. I didn't even keep it. I hid it. It was like I had to hold something back, something in reserve. Until I was sure—

Sure of what?

I don't know. It was stupid. I mean, it was like—I don't know. It was like I couldn't let him go. Homer, I mean. Do you think maybe that's why he's haunting me?

I think we've drunk too much Scotch to be discussing this, she says. Listen, Larry, your father was a driven man. There was a hole in the middle of his life—a black hole—it sucked all the love out of our marriage—it sucked away the love you kids needed more than anything. It's just *like* him to come back from the dead. That last page—what did it say? How *does* the story end?

I don't know. I can't remember. I don't think I read it. I was in a state. I hid it—maybe it's still there—where I hid it. I don't know if it matters...

Get some sleep, Larry.

When I finally stretch out on the sofa, sleep falls on me like a tree. I sleep hard and long and when I wake daylight streams in and both Walter and Liz have gone to work. There is coffee and *The New York Times*. I sit in the sunshine and drink the coffee, read the news. Thirteen stories below, people shuffle their double parked cars from one side of the street to the other. I wonder, can you get a flight from here to Moose Jaw?

The phone rings. I think I should let the machine get it, but then I wonder if it might be Bonnie so I pick it up. It's Walter.

Hey, Larry. Liz asked me to make a couple of calls. Crazy as it sounds—I think she's right. The pair of them *have* been making the rounds. The strange part is—they seem to have made quite an impression. Top people have actually been *talking* to them. These are houses that get *billions* of words of unsolicited prose shovelled in over the transom every week—and just shovel it back out. *Nobody* just walks up to the door and goes straight upstairs like these two have been doing. They must be something else. Apparently the kid carries the manuscript in a locked briefcase   chained to his wrist. It's brilliant, really. These people fight off manuscripts with both hands. But tell them you've got one—

only they can't see it—I don't know, Larry, it's getting them in the door, creating a wave. The strangest part of the whole business is that they're making no bones about the kid being illiterate. I guess the book is supposed to be some sort of revealed truth.

Bizarre, I say.

Scary is what it is. Just makes me glad I've got a real job. I mean—the grapevine's already got this as big as *The Celestine Prophesy*. And nobody's actually read it yet!

I read some of it, I say. It didn't read like a bestseller to me.

I've read some of Homer's earlier books, Larry. Liz sent them to me—back when we were still carrying on at a distance. I passed them around—but I knew they wouldn't go anywhere. He had *bushels* of talent but he couldn't write a *novel*. I told her she should encourage him to try short stories. There were brilliant *scenes* there…

Maybe he took your advice. He did write some stories—Katherine sold some of them to little magazines, under a pen-name. Now she's put them into a book and sold it to a publisher in Vancouver.

Good for her. I look forward to reading it. But this manuscript-on-a-chain trick—I guess I'll believe it when it comes out in hard-cover. Glad I got out of the business.

I appreciate your help with this, Walter. You didn't happen to hear where they might be staying?

That's the upshot, Larry—seems you're too late. Rumour has it they flew to L.A. this morning, talking movie deals. Listen, I've got to get back to work. I thought you should know.

A couple of minutes later my mother calls from her office. I relate what I've heard from Walter.

What now, Larry? she says. Don't tell me you're off to L.A.?

At least stay for dinner.

No, I say. No and no. I'm not going to L.A. but I won't stay either. That's why I called. I'm catching the next bus to Montréal.

Montréal?

I'm going to stop off in Shawville on my way home. I think it's time I looked up Mr. Leo Knotts.

Be careful, Larry. If this character *did* kill Homer—what's to stop him doing the same to you?

I'll be careful.

What about the book?

Fuck the book! Fuck Olivia! Fuck little brother Y. I don't know anybody in Hollywood and I don't think I want to. It's all smoke and mirrors, anyway, Mother. If they can pull off their scam in Hollywood—then fuck Hollywood, too. I want to know what *really* happened to my father.

Just be careful, Larry.

I'll be careful.

You'd better be. Bonnie needs you, you know.

I hope so. But I've got to do this.

Call me. Oh, and Larry—if it should turn out that somehow Bonnie is right—if Homer *is* still alive—tell him for me that he's an asshole.

I walk to the Port Authority Bus Terminal. New York is too much—unbelievable. Hasn't *really* changed a damn since it scared and thrilled and delighted and disgusted me when Liz and Homer brought us here as kids, to visit the museums and ride the carousel in Central Park. The energy at street level is still awesome. I feel terribly alive and sober and unafraid.

I take the bus because I've had enough of flying. I want to stay close to the earth, to feel it solid under my feet, or at least under the throbbing wheels of the Greyhound. I take a seat near the back. Click it back—stretch out. But I don't sleep.

Walter, down in the East Village, is doing what he can. When my mother met him he was successful, respected, well-off—stressed-out. The stress nearly killed him. Now he feeds the homeless, helps the hopeless—a life of service. Obvious, isn't it?

There was a time, when I was young, when I thought *I* was here to help. To fight for peace, to feed the world, to find the cure. I remember I wanted to be a brain surgeon—saving lives with my confident, unerring fingers—until I puked, dissecting a dead frog in Biology. I remember I was going to go to jail to stop the war in Vietnam—but my mother took a job in Canada and I swallowed my pride and went along for the ride.

I was going to seek enlightenment but when I dropped acid I found out it was already here. Spent the rest of my life trying to remember what it was I was trying to forget—or something...

A good carpenter. Top of my apprenticeship class. (But *I*

188

knew I was faking it.) Journeyman's certificate, union card. (Faking it.) I can build anything; I know the building code; I understand the principles of structure and design—but for *what*? To build banks and offices and warehouses? Okay—so I *have* built a couple of hospitals and day-care centers, too.

I've loved Bonnie, and Adam, done my best for *them*, haven't I? I'm a nice guy—people like me. Don't they? What the hell am I *doing* here, alone on this bus? The windows of the bus are smoked, the day is dull. Dirty snow in the ditches. What's the game, Homer? What do you want from me? Alive—dead—somewhere in the unclear unclean places in between? What is it you need from *me*—the son you never trusted, not for a minute, not for a moment—the son you betrayed, abandoned, from the first moment, then turned on, blamed? I know it *now*, damn it. Is *this* the moment you've been driving me toward?

Somewhere along the road I cross a border, pass through a wall, the mirror dissolves— ripples only on the surface… I come to myself, realizing that I am different. Something passes through me—a moment of darkness—full of bristling light. I know the feeling, intimately, but I am not sure it is not death…

Darkness—not enough blood to the brain—everything sucking away. Then slipping back again, clearer, more solid, apparently…

Somewhere on the dark late highway we stop for Homer's ghost. Still got his damn rain gear on, though the air is full of snow. He sinks into the seat beside me, smelling like the sea.

It's true then, I say.

No, Larry. Not all of it.

Why, Homer?

There was no other way, Larry. I thought you'd understand.

Don't give me that crap, Homer. There's always options.

Keep believing that, Larry.

I try to grab him, but he is only a ghost—only a dream of a ghost.

I rent a car in Montréal. Good thing I've got plenty of credit. Never used it much before. Like my father—I prefer cash.

I am tired of being a passenger. I have the unusual feeling that I am finally in control. I speak French with the woman at the car rental place—confident, articulate. The whole transaction has a dreamlike feel. Like dreams where you can fly, or play the violin. I know I don't really *know* this much French—but somehow the words come.

The car is an automatic. It follows the road. I am very calm. Maybe I have just never been quite this close to the edge. A strange feeling in my chest—a constriction, but no pain—a supreme absence of pain—an emptiness...

Very calm. What would you call this feeling? Presence of mind? The car is automatic. The road knows where it goes. The car is automatic. So am I.

Everything is covered with snow. The signs are in a strange language. Can it be the same one I recently pretended to speak so trippingly off the tongue? But that was already long ago—this present evaporates that past and I am losing the edge...

This is not a movie. I follow the river. Should have asked for a standard—should have rented something with some *balls*—blown into town in a cloud. Losing the edge, already.

I stop at a pharmacy in Aylmer and buy a pair of scissors and a disposable razor. Better this way. Slip into town unnoticed. Automatic. At a self-service station near Quyon, I buy gas and ask the cashier for the key to the washroom. I take the beard off first—snipping it close with the scissors—then trying to work up some sort of lather with the liquid soap. It's a painful, messy business, but not life-threatening. I shave almost as well as I speak French, maybe.

The hair seems easier at first—I just snip off the pony tail. Then it starts to get technical. I'm beginning to wonder if maybe I've made a serious error in judgement when someone knocks on the door.

You okay in there? It's the young cashier. She doesn't sound angry. A bit scared, maybe—doesn't want to find me with a needle hanging out of my arm.

I'm fine, I say, frantically mopping up my clippings and flushing them down the toilet. I drop the pony-tail in the trash—then fish it out again. When I return the key, I'm still holding it in my hand. The cashier sees it and giggles—blushes.

Why'd you go and cut your hair off? she says.

I have to be someone else, I say, blushing myself.

Are you like—running away from something?

No, I say. Running—but not away.

What are you going to do with it? She indicates my hair, which I still hold like a bouquet.

I don't know. I couldn't bring myself to just throw it in the trash. It's been a part of me for a long time. You want it?

She blushes again. I couldn't, she says.

What do you think? I ask her, spinning on my heel to let her see the back.

Not bad. Well, not *really* bad, eh?

Hey, I'm a carpenter—not a barber.

191

Here, she says—putting down her book and holding out her hand for the scissors.

The trick is to freeze to the moment. Our breath is mist. The night is cold, clear—stars as sharp as nails. Denise moves around me and the scissors make crisp little sounds around my ears. We haven't introduced ourselves, but I know her name because it is embroidered over her pocket. She has to stop once to take twenty-five dollars from a trucker. I study my reflection in the glass. Somebody I knew once—maybe—but older. When the trucker is gone she takes my severed pony-tail and uses it to whisk the hair off my shoulders.

These scissors are shit, she says. I'm off in like half-an-hour—if you want to wait around you could come over to my place and I can give you a real haircut, eh?

Thank you very much for the offer, I say. This is real enough for me.

Real enough. The late night highway. Here and there they already have Christmas lights up. Shawville is dead as the day after doomsday. Not a dog—not a squirrel—not a breath of breeze whipping the snow around on Main Street. A flickering street-light—the flashing red of the single traffic signal. I park behind the hotel, lock the car, shoulder my pack and walk around to the front.

Nobody at reception. Nobody anywhere. I bend over the desk and open the register. Only one guest registered. I am standing there like a zombie with deja vu, just staring at the entry — *Room 213 / Ms. A. Hamilton, Nanaimo, BC*—when the night clerk appears. A different guy.

192

Where's Raul? I say, knowing that wasn't the other guy's name, exactly. He knows who I mean.

Ralph? It's his night off.

Can I get a room for one night? Number two-fifteen, if it's available? He looks at me strangely, so I say, I stayed there once before. Enjoyed the view.

He looks at me *really* strangely (*View? What view?*) but I just smile and sign the book—*Loki Thorvaldson, Foam Lake, Saskatchewan*. I'm standing there feeling clever until I realize this means I can't use my credit card. I clean out my wallet—just make it. I leave him recounting the change, pocket my remaining forty-three cents and take the key.

The view from 215 is of a darkened alley full of snow and trash. Olivia's room—last time. It's impossible, but somehow it seems her scent lingers. The room is cold but I crank up the baseboard heat and as it ticks and moves the air I swear a tang of sweet vanilla rises like a nostalgic aftertaste.

Get a grip on the present moment, Loki. Presence of mind. Presence of body. Get a grip.

Ouch. Not so hard.

For a long time I don't know what it is that isn't. Then I get it—no coughing. The hacker upstairs must have moved out—or died. I can't sleep. Too quiet—just the heater ticking like a metronome so slow time starts to gel. Wide awake. Presence of mind. On the other side of this wall, Art Humble is sleeping like a baby. Or is he? Is he even *he*? How does this unlikely character manage to turn up everywhere I go? Have I been wrong all along? Could he really be two people after all? Remembering Artemis

Hamilton at Homer's memorial, I give my head a shake. But then—at Zanzu's place with Olivia that morning—the light was poor—Zanzu did most of the talking. But maybe there *was* something different about the creature who crouched there—grinning—hiding behind the smoke-screen of Zanzu's Camels. Could Arthur really *have* a cousin Artemis, and sometimes he impersonates her? Which one of them *is* on the other side of that wall, then? *Both*?

Me, I'm here alone with my imagination and the smell of a long-gone lawyer.

I decide it's not too late to call Adam. Three hours earlier there. He picks it up on the second ring.

Hey, Larry. You still in New York?

No. I'm in Shawville.

Shit—I think Bonnie's trying to get in touch with you.

What do you mean? Where is she? Did she go to Moose Jaw?

I don't think so. She only stayed one night here. I don't actually know *where* she is now. But she called Speed Avenue and talked to Sylvie, and Sylvie told her you'd gone to New York— and she asked Sylvie for your mother's fax number.

Her *fax* number?

That's what Sylvie said. Too bad you didn't hang out in New York. What's shaking in Shawville?

Good question. Nothing, probably. I just have to check out a couple of things here—then I'm heading home. Tell Bonnie I love her. If she calls. Tell her I'll be home soon. If she calls.

You okay, Larry?

Sure. Fine.

Too late to call New York. Catch them in the morning before they go to work. Don't have Liz's office number—have to get up and call her before seven-thirty. Should have brought my travel alarm. Call the night clerk and ask for a wake-up call? Not that I'll sleep. Too wired. Presence of fucking mind.

In the dream box there are three elements. Inside—outside—the box itself. Maybe not elements? Elephants?

When I wake and stand in front of the window I feel like a man who has finally been allowed to take off the blindfold. The sun is sharp as daggers off the fresh snow; the trash in the alley is gone under a glittering blanket of puffy flakes. I've slept like the dead, but now I'm wide awake for sure. So what the hell am I doing here?

Can't get a dial tone on the room telephone so I dress quickly and sneak down to the pay phone. Get my mother's machine. I don't leave a message.

Nobody around. Back up the stairs. The chamberperson is running water and whistling in Room 214, and as I walk past her cart I notice the pass-key lying there on top of a pile of clean towels. Without stopping to think, I pick it up and step across the hall. As I open the door of Room 213, I am fully prepared to confront Art Humble—or Art Hamilton—or both?—in bed, on the john, even sitting there waiting for me. The room is empty. Either the bed has already been made-up or it wasn't slept in. The door to the bathroom is open—no one. I toss the key back on the pile of towels and slip inside, close the door behind me.

I check the closets—a single locked suitcase. She (or he—or they) will be back. No toothbrush or shaving things in the bathroom.

I get down on my knees and open the cabinet under the vanity. I check my pockets, and my heart sinks. Like a man without a blindfold I stare at screw heads. I remember a million years ago

196

or so, handing my Swiss Army knife to Bonnie to clean that fish. I can see her now—carefully drying the blade—folding it—slipping it into the pocket of her jeans.

I check my pockets again. I check the room. Must be *something* I can fashion to fit a fucking flathead screw. Do I dare to prop the door open and zip down the street to Canadian Tire for a screwdriver? What if the chamberperson sees me? What if Art or Art comes back while I'm gone?

I try again. The corner of a credit card is too flimsy—a thin dime too thick. The only remotely screwdriver-blade-shaped thing I can find about my person is the little metal pull of the zipper of my fly. YKK. What the bloody hell—I've come this far. I climb out of my pants and get down on my knees again and try it but it has this little hump in the middle that makes it just too thick for the slot. I'm squatting there, wondering if maybe I could hone it down on something—like maybe the rough under-edge of the cistern cover—when I hear the click of a key slipping into a lock.

I have time to get my pants back on, but not to pull them all the way up, before Artemis Hamilton pushes open the bathroom door—with the barrel of a handgun.

Nice haircut, Loki.

I fumble to get my pants over my knees but she raises the pistol and points it into my eyes and says, Leave them.

I have never stared down the barrel of a gun before. Why does it feel so damn familiar? I let my pants drop back to my ankles, raise my hands.

Nice legs, too, she says. Too bad about the knees.

She steps into the bathroom and closes the door behind her. I can't imagine what I was thinking. *This* Artemis Hamilton is no skinny private dick in drag—she is unequivocally female—her breath and sweat and voice and body language all drool with a humid femaleness in the suddenly stifling space.

She rummages in her handbag, comes up with something that looks like a cigarette case, but when she holds it to her eye it flashes at me—a camera. She slips it back in the handbag, rummages some more and produces a set of stainless steel handcuffs and a roll of duct tape. The hand holding the gun never wavers—the length of its barrel is never for an instant visible to both my eyes at once. She has the key to the handcuffs on a chain around her neck. She opens them both, tosses them to me. I drop them.

Wake up, Loki. Do you think you can stay with me on this?

I'll try, but look—

I don't have to look very far, she says. You think this is the first time in my life I've come home to find a half-naked rapist in my bathroom?

It's not? I mean—I'm not—I just—wanted to talk to you.

Fine. We'll talk. But first pick up the cuffs—put one on your left wrist—feed the other through the toilet seat and put it on your right wrist.

For Christ's sake—

She lowers the gun, points it at my crotch.

Does this have anything to do with what happened at Bone Island, I say, because—

She cocks the pistol and I shrug and handcuff myself to the oak toilet seat. The cuffs feel solid enough, but I notice the toilet seat has a hairline crack near the back.

Don't even think about it, Loki, she says. Sit down.

How?

Use your imagination.

I kick one leg free of my pants and swing it over the chain, sit down on the toilet with my hands chained between my thighs.

Good, she says. She strips a yard of duct tape off the roll but doesn't tear it off. Kneeling by my feet, she wriggles the cold steel barrel of the pistol under the elastic of my briefs at the inside of my thigh and nestles it gently under my penis—probing into the softness between my testicles.

Hold still, she says, unnecessarily. There is very little colour in the knuckle of her trigger finger.

With her free hand she wraps the tape around my ankles—two—three—four wraps. She strips back more of the roll and then bounces it off the baseboard behind the toilet, retrieves it on the other side. As she reaches for it the gun digs painfully into my right testicle and I squeal.

Sorry, she says, but she doesn't relieve the pressure and by the time she has repeated this trick four times—securing my ankles firmly to the base of the toilet—the steel of the pistol barrel no longer feels cold. Finally she tears the tape. Stands up, steps back, sets the roll and the pistol beside the wash basin on the vanity.

That was probably your best chance, she says. A shot to the testicles is painful but rarely fatal. Besides, the gun's not even loaded. In fact—it's not even a real gun.

That's what I figured, I say.

Oh yeah? How'd you figure that?

Well. I've been waiting for it to turn up. The replica handgun *somebody* supposedly pulled on Homer, trying to rob his bookstore. Homer took the gun away from whoever it was—or bought it or something—but it never turned up in his stuff.

Okay—you knew it was a fake. So why did you let me tie you up, then? Not overly clever, Loki.

I *suspected* it was fake. I wasn't *sure*. And maybe I was hoping that if I let you feel like you had the upper hand—you might relax a bit and tell me what the fuck is really going on. What *real-*

ly happened to Homer? What has Leo Knotts got to do with it? Are you *really* Art Humble's cousin or is Art Humble really just one of *your* disguises?

Shit.

What.

I went and tied you to the toilet. I'll have to piss in the sink.

My room key is in the pocket of my pants. You can use my washroom in there if you want.

While you check out just how firmly that toilet is bolted down? What am I going to do with you, Loki?

Tell me the truth?

But you seem to know so much already. Suppose you tell *me* what *you* think.

I think Leo Knotts killed Homer, I lie. I'm not sure why, but I think it had something to do with the book. And I'm beginning to think maybe *you* helped him.

You're just saying that. What were you really doing here in my bathroom, Larry? Looking for something? This was *your* room last time, wasn't it? Did you maybe leave something behind?

My eyes flash to the doors of the vanity—I can't help it. She raises her eyebrows, bends enough to open the doors and peer inside.

Not *overly* clever, Loki. An access panel. Shall we have a look? There's a screwdriver in my suitcase. Back in a sec. Don't go anywhere.

She opens the bathroom door, moves over to the closet. While she is fiddling with the lock on her suitcase the telephone rings. She gives me a sharp glance as she crosses to answer it, but when she picks it up she moves away and turns her back so I can't hear what she is saying. She talks for a long time—her words indecipherable but her voice palpably intense.

I consider the indignity of my situation, cast about for some means of escape. I can *just* reach the tape between my ankles with the fingers of my right hand. If my nails were sharper—if I had something sharp I could hold between my fingers…Nothing in reach. Unless—I lean over and slip my glasses off. I pop one lens out of the frame with my thumb and lift my weight enough to wiggle the little dish of hardened glass between the handcuff chain and the porcelain bowl. I lift my weight as high as I can and come down hard on the seat. These hardened lenses *will* break— I dropped my glasses on a concrete slab once and one shattered. But I don't have this one positioned quite right—it shoots out— bounces off the shower curtain and clatters into the tub.

Art Hamilton turns and glares at me, but only for a moment. I grin, stupidly, and the moment she turns away I pop the other lens. What the hell—I place this one more carefully and when I bounce down on the seat, it shatters with a small pop—like a snail under a boot. Art's still in there—talking. I manage to retrieve an inch-long shard of glass and I stick my left hand right in the toilet to give my right more chain—start hacking and sawing at the tape between my ankles.

In the other room, Art raises her voice, but the only words I make out are obscenities and—once—Zanzu's name. I concentrate on my work and I'm slicing the last sticky threads (and only bleeding a little) when I don't hear her voice any more. And then there she is—standing in the doorway, shaking her head, looking down at me.

The chamberperson raps twice on the door from the corridor and opens it with her pass key. *Housekeeping*, she sings, her voice bright. And then—Oh, excuse me—

I grab the toilet seat with both hands—launch myself off the commode with every gram of fast-twitch muscle in my frame. Unfortunately, the tape—while cut clean through—still clings about my ankles. I kick my left foot free but the right stays tangled behind and I pitch sideways—face first—into the side of the tub. The toilet seat doesn't break, either, so I just about yank my hands off at the wrist—not to mention nearly dislocating my shoulders. And taking both elbows hard in the groin.

As I bounce off the tub and hit the floor, the rusty flange-bolts finally break away and the whole toilet lifts and tips and falls on top of me. The cold water line shears just behind the shut-off valve and a bolt of ice cold water starts to peel the paper off the opposite wall. Tank and bowl empty over me, but the excess water flows away quickly at the broken flange. So—trapped, damaged and humiliated as I may be—I am in little actual danger of drowning.

Artemis Hamilton shakes her head. She puts down the screwdriver and picks up the gun—waves it casually at the flabbergasted chamberperson. Better come in and close that door, she says.

The chamberperson looks like she is about seventeen and trying hard not to pee in her pants. She obeys. Mr. Thorvaldson and I have been having some trouble with the plumbing, says Art. You understand?

The girl shakes her head.

Doesn't matter. Unfortunately, Mr. Thorvaldson and I have to be going. Too bad. You'll look after this little problem for us, I hope?

The girl looks from the gun to the broken toilet—to the rush of water—to me, soaking wet in my underwear, still chained to the broken toilet.

I'm sorry, she says.

Just keep it out of the papers. No cops. You don't want us coming back or you'll have real trouble. This should cover the damage.

She pulls a roll of those same old fifties out of her handbag—starts to peel some off—stuff them in the pockets of the girl's smock.

That's funny money, I say.

Are you going to take the word of a man chained to a toilet?

The gun's a fake, too, I say.

Art shoots a hole in the floor beside my foot. The roar of the small gun is deafening in the enclosed space. I didn't want to have to do that, she says, stuffing the money back in her purse. She takes the handcuff key off the chain around her neck and hands it to the girl.

Unlock those cuffs and get that toilet off him. We've got to get going.

Sorry, I say. She *told* me it was a fake. The girl's hands are shaking so badly she can hardly get the key in the hole. Relax, I say. She's crazy but I don't think she'll hurt you.

Shut up, Loki. What's your name, sweet thing?

Lorelli. Please, I think we should try to turn off that water.

Here, I say, pushing the toilet off my leg. I pick up the lid of the tank and pound the broken pipe flat with it, slowing the flow to a spluttering spray and finally to a hissing trickle.

Art is shaking her head again.

I'm a carpenter, I say, not a fucking plumber.

Chain yourself to that carpenter, Lorelli—then give me back that key. I'm afraid you'll have to come with us.

We take my rental car. Art has let me put my pants back on, but they are as drenched as the rest of me. Fortunately the rental car has a good heater.

You drive, Loki.

I'm not supposed to drive without my glasses, I say.

Okay—you drive, Lorelli.

I don't know how to drive.

Shitcity. Okay—Loki drives—you tell him if anything's coming.

Art sits in the back and keeps the gun at the back of my neck. Lorelli sits in the passenger seat, keeping her left hand on the wheel, just above my right, to which it is chained.

You'll find Loki isn't such a bad guy when he dries out a little, says Art. But don't go and fall for him. He's a married man.

Why did you lie to me about the gun? I say.

It's what I do.

Is this like a lover's quarrel or something? asks Lorelli.

Art laughs so hard it is almost like barking. Loki has some funny ideas, she says, but not *that* funny. He thinks I'm really a man in drag. What do *you* think, honey?

I think you're both crazy.

You should have kept your big mouth shut and let her take the money, Loki.

My name's not Loki, I say.

Loki isn't even sure of his own name any more. He thinks Leo Knotts killed his father. You know Leo Knotts, Lorelli?

No.

You're a lucky girl. Leo's not a nice man. You're much better off being chained to Loki here. Leo has no scruples. He'd chew your hand off at the wrist in a minute.

Why'd he kill Loki's father?

He didn't. Loki is mistaken about all sorts of things.

He was *there*, I say. Margaret told me he was *there*.

Shut up and drive, Loki.

Where?

Zanzu's place. You know Zanzu, Lorelli?

I've heard about her.

Zanzu and Loki's dad had a little fling—a long time ago. Loki thinks that's why Leo killed his dad. Not because it happened—because his dad went and wrote a book about it. Loki believes all sorts of things. Would you kill somebody because of a book, Lorelli?

No.

Me neither. But Loki comes from a *literary* family. They're different. Me—I'm not even sure there ever even *was* such a book.

There was a book, I say.

Really? I know your father gave you a parcel that he *said* had a book in it. I also know he asked you not to open it. You didn't go and open it, did you, Loki?

No, I lie.

So maybe it wasn't a book at all. Maybe it was blank paper—or old newspapers or funny money or something?

Why would he do that?

Maybe it was just a diversion. Misdirection. Something to mislead your attention from what was really going on.

What if I *had* opened the package?

Did you?

Maybe.

I knew it. I can read you like a book, Loki.

Lorelli says, So like—what happened to the book?

My kid brother took it to Hollywood, I say.

Art laughs. They won't buy it in Hollywood, though, you know why, Lorelli? Maybe a little something is missing. Maybe Loki held a little something back—didn't you, Loki? Loki is the god of mischief—did you know that, Lorelli?

Yes.

My name's Larry, I say.

Y's horse, Rhona, stares at us over the fence at Zanzu's place. At least I think it's Rhona. Everything's sort of soft and fuzzy without my glasses. Zanzu's station wagon is not in the lot. She had to go up to Wolf Lake to feed Leo's dogs, says Art. The kid was looking after them till he fucked off with that lawyer.

Let the girl go, I say. Can't you see she's petrified?

I'm okay, says Lorelli.

She's okay, says Art. Use your brain, Loki. If I let her go she'll have the cops on us so fast we won't have time to blink. You want Bonnie reading in the morning paper about how you turned up chained to my toilet without your pants on?

She'll understand, I say.

No, she says. You wouldn't keep your big mouth shut and now our Lorelli knows too much.

You're going to kill me, aren't you? Lorelli is very pale, but she speaks calmly.

Not unless I have to, dear. But you understand I can't just let you go until I have a little insurance.

Insurance?

Nothing serious, sweetheart. A couple of embarrassing photos of you with Romeo here—maybe a discrete tattoo. How'd you like to have *I love Loki* tattooed in flames on your butt? Go on, get inside.

Zanzu's stove is cold. I am shaking as I make the fire—Lorelli standing close since we are still joined at the wrist.

Please, she says. I won't say anything—I promise, eh? I didn't understand a thing you were talking about, anyway.

Relax, says Art. It won't be so bad. You won't have to actually *do* it with Loki, just fake it—for the camera.

She opens the fridge, finds beer, opens one for each of us. Lorelli and I sit on the narrow bed. I crowd as close to the fire as I can, but I'm still wet through and my teeth are chattering.

I couldn't, says Lorelli, when Art hands her the beer.

Go ahead, kid. It'll help you to relax.

Honest, I won't tell *anybody*. Please let me go. I can keep a secret. When my cousin Denise got pregnant and had to get an abortion, I never told *nobody*.

Your cousin Denise?

That works at the PetroCan in Quyon.

Denise is your *cousin*? I say. *Denise* gave me this haircut.

You know Denise? Shit. Please, *please*, don't tell her I told you, okay?

You aren't doing your case much good, I say. Take the beer.

She's not really going to tattoo me, is she?

God knows. She's taken this whole thing pretty hard.

What whole thing?

She used to work for my father.

Poor Loki has me confused with someone else, says Art. I

used to be in love with his father, but I never worked for him.

She's lying again.

Shut up and drink your beer, Loki. You don't know shit.

Tell me shit, then.

Lorelli drinks her bottle of beer in three long swallows. I notice that she *does* look a little like her cousin Denise—only prettier. I wonder when Zanzu will get back. Art laughs and opens Lorelli another beer.

Zanzu has most of a dozen beer in her fridge. We drink them all. Zanzu's bathroom is a composting toilet behind a red silk curtain. Art uses it but keeps the gun in sight. Then, when it is our turn, she won't take the cuffs off, so Lorelli and I get to take turns standing outside the curtain.

After this morning, I don't trust Loki around toilets, says Art. Lorelli goes first, and pees for a long time. Something poignantly intimate about it. When it finally is my turn, my bladder gets shy. The beer has gone right through me and burns to finish the trip but standing there with both of them waiting outside the curtain—I just can't unclench the valves. All I manage is a dribble.

What's he *doing* in there, Lorelli? Jerking off?

I can feel Lorelli blush right through the chain. More valves clench—the ones which let the blood escape from my dangling prick. It begins to swell a little and the burning in my bladder takes on a vaguely erotic edge. I try to quiet all my urges, to relax, to imagine myself alone in the center of the earth, but the harder I try the less my body is fooled. Finally I coax a brief, almost ejaculatory squirt—unnaturally loud in the water-less toilet.

Don't squeeze it so hard, Loki, calls Art. Lorelli giggles. She's drunk more beer than me and Art together. To my dismay, I feel the flesh between my fingers growing thicker, lifting away from the bowl. I give up—stuff it back in my pants—zip up.

Thought you had to go, says Art.

So did I, I say.

Lorelli giggles. More beer, she says.

Lying back on Zanzu's narrow bed, the heat in my bladder is a dull roar, quietly drowning out my other hurts—the bruises on my forehead and knee and shoulder, the cuts on my fingers, the golf ball of knotted flesh where the toilet landed on my ankle. My nose, reminded suddenly of Duncan's fist by the side of the bath-tub.

Lorelli is drunk. Art unlocked the handcuffs just long enough to feed the chain through the oak rails of the headboard, so we lie—side by side—each with an arm stretched out. The space between us has dwindled with Zanzu's supply of beer. The fire is really putting out now. It gets very warm in the little house; we steam in our still damp clothes. Lorelli is sloppy drunk and soft against me and I hurt almost all over but somehow still have a throbbing hard-on trapped in my pants and Artie Hamilton (still nursing her first beer?) watches the window—perfectly androgynous in concentration—terrifyingly calm.

Were you really in love with Homer? I ask her, just to make conversation, to try and take my mind off my multiple discomforts. Art shoots me a look, then fastens her gaze on the window again, checks her watch.

Neither of us knew it at the time, she says.

Why not?

He had the hots for that lawyer. What *is* it about her?

Who's Homer? Lorelli says. What lawyer?

Art ignores her. I was young, she says. Confused. I didn't

expect to fall in love—certainly not with someone like *him*. I thought it must be something else.

When did you know? I ask her.

When Leo Knotts cut my prick off and fed it to his dogs, she says.

That's *gross*, says Lorelli.

Leo Knotts cut—

I remember thinking—even through the pain—that if I lived through this maybe Homer would be able to love me now.

Leo cut your—fed it to his—

I think I'm going to be sick, says Lorelli. Leaning across me she pukes beer and breakfast all over the rug.

Jesus galloping Christ! I say.

Shit, says Art.

Sorry, says Lorelli. Can we take those pictures soon? I want to go home.

Zanzu's gonna kill me, says Art, gathering up the pukey rug and tossing it out into the snow.

Lorelli is crying. Art standing at the window, checking her watch. When the phone rings she pounces.

Bloody hell, woman, where *are* you? No—everything's fine. What? He what? Jesus, Mary and Joseph! *No! Don't* come here! I'll meet you somewhere. No, you tell *me* where. Okay, I'll be there in—checking her watch—twenty minutes. No. Don't talk to *anybody*. Don't panic—I'm on my way.

Artemis Hamilton hangs up the phone, unplugs it and puts it in her purse. She looks at us on the bed, shakes her head, hands Lorelli her nearly empty bottle of beer. Don't go anywhere, she says, and before we can protest she is out the door and gone. We hear my rental car start up and turn out of the drive.

I got to pee again, says Lorelli.

Me too.

Maybe we can break the chain, she says.

I doubt it. But maybe if we saw at the rail we can cut through it.

We try. It is hard to get a good sawing rhythm going—Lorelli is very drunk and I can't pull as hard as I'd like for fear of breaking her skinny wrist. The polished links of alloy steel just slide over the finished oak. We wear some of the varnish off but we'll wear our wrists through before the oak.

I think I'm gonna just pee, says Lorelli. Do you mind?

Maybe we can move the bed, I say.

To the toilet?

No. But I can see something sticking out from under the back of the stove—I'm pretty sure it's the handle of a hatchet. If we could turn the bed I might be able to reach it with my foot.

How can we move the bed if we can't even get off it?

If we push our feet against the wall—maybe we can shove it over, I say. We wriggle around until we are both able to get some purchase with bent knees. Here goes nothing, I say. On three. One—two—

We push off the wall with desperate drunken enthusiasm and the bed-frame—instead of sliding—starts to tip. In a moment we are going over. Lorelli lets out a shriek and grabs me as we hit the floor. The bed comes crashing over on top of us.

We end up squashed and tangled tight together, Lorelli on top, clinging to me like death. When I feel the hot rush all over my belly I think for one terrible moment that she is hurt—broken—hemorrhaging, but in the stifling space my nose quickly tells me different. As Lorelli pees and pees all over me I sigh and piss myself.

Lorelli giggles.

Somehow we manage to get untangled. We roll over and lift the bed on our backs and try to tortoise our way closer, but the bed frame jams firmly between the desk and table. I take my sock off and try to reach the hatchet with my foot, but even wriggling and squirming and stretching every sinew—and pulling on the handcuffs till Lorelli cries out in pain—I can't quite touch it with my toes.

I start to cry.

Hey, says Lorelli. It was a good idea.

I stop crying. Are you wearing panty-hose? I ask her.

Yes.

Take them off.

She blushes, but she does it. I ain't on the pill or anything, she says, struggling to work the soggy tights off her ankles with her one free hand.

Good, I say. Give them to me.

I wring the piss out of them and fashion a crude lariat. One end I knot securely around my ankle—the loop I grasp between my two longest toes. By sheer luck I am able to lasso the hatchet on the fifth or sixth kick. I ease the loop tight and then carefully pull the hatchet toward us.

Cool, says Lorelli.

Cover your eyes, I say, when I finally have the hatchet in my hand. The blade is dull and whacking at the chain only blunts it more, so I have a go at the rail. I'm not so good with my left hand and for at least ten minutes we eat chips and splinters, but finally I chop through and we are free—of the bed, if not of each other.

I help Lorelli put her soggy panty-hose back on.

It is maybe a quarter mile to the next house. I try not to think about what I'm going to say when we get there. Two vehicles pass

212

us, and Lorelli tries to flag them down, but they don't stop. By the time we reach the next house our pissy clothing is starting to freeze and we are shaking like a couple of drunks with DTs.

The yard is full of toy trucks and climbing toys and pallets and pieces of engines and the open carport is full of tools and scrap. The house is a low-slung unfinished bungalow on a concrete block foundation. No sign of life. We ring and bang and try the door. Nobody home. The door is locked.

Near the back of the carport I uncover a set of tanks and acetylene torches. Haven't played with one of these suckers since I was an apprentice, but I figure at this point if I blow us up it will be almost a relief. I crank on all the valves and strike a flame.

You do know what you're doing, eh? says Lorelli.

I hope so.

I adjust the oxygen till the flame is a wedge of glittering blue.

Turns out the back door of the house is open. It is very warm inside—and stinks of creosote and cat shit and fried meat. We hold our wrists under the cold water till the pain subsides. The cat—a big black bruiser—hisses at us from the top of the refrigerator. A crocheted blanket hangs over the back of a threadbare sofa and Lorelli wraps herself up and sinks into the cushions.

You gonna call the cops, Loki?

Yeah, sure.

I find the phone and dial—keeping my thumb on the button. Hello, I say, into the buzzing receiver. *Oui, bonjour,* I say, remembering that I am still in Québec. *Parlez-vous Anglais?* I try, then launch into a mumbled, garbled version of our recent ordeal. I give some sort of address and hang up.

They're sending a car for us, I tell Lorelli, but she is fast asleep.

I find the bathroom, strip off my soggy stinky clothes, sponge myself off. I find dry clothing in the bedroom closet. The pants are a tad short and way too big at the waist, but I find a leather belt and cinch it tight. I pull on as many shirts and sweaters as I can wriggle into and still move. I rinse the piss off my keys and wallet—dry them on a tea towel. I stuff my own clothes in the garbage.

Lorelli is snoring. I get another blanket from the bedroom and spread it over her, then slip out the back door.

I walk out to the highway and hitch a ride as far as Ladysmith with a beer truck. He's delivering to the Hotel, right there at the Lac du Loup turn-off. I decide to stop in and use the phone.

I dial my mother's number—get her machine.

Hi, Mother, I say to the listening silence. It's me, calling to see if you've heard from Bonnie. Nowhere you can reach me right now so I guess I'll have to try again. If she calls you—tell her I'm heading home.

I hang up. And stand there, wondering why I'm *not* heading home. Why even now, after all that's gone down, I'm reaching across the wires to lie to the one person I *really* owe the truth. Wondering—*knowing* that Leo Knotts isn't home, that Zanzu went out there just this morning to feed his penis-eating dogs— why the bloody hell I'm standing here at this cross-roads, trying to decide whether to have a sandwich before I step back out the door and see if I can hitch a ride to Wolf Lake.

A small grey haggard-looking man pushes open the door. He gives me an odd look—like maybe my clothes are familiar but not my face—then moves past me to the bar. Hey, John, he calls to the heavy-set man behind the bar. You hear what happened to Leo Knotts?

Leo Knotts? says the bartender. Delmer Knotts's cousin?

That's him. The biker, eh? Used to run with that hippie woman has that tattoo place down the Seventh Line.

Yeah? What about him?

Son-of-a-bitch is dead, eh? They're sayin' his own dogs ate him, by the Jeez! I guess there weren't a fuck of a lot left of him by the time the cops got there, eh?

No shit? says the bartender. I heard about them dogs.

Not quite sure how I got here to the airport. I know there was a ride in a station wagon, a long incoherent conversation in broken French with the driver—who was either a lapsed priest or a born-again fisherman.

The woman at the ticket counter won't sell me a ticket. Her machine rejects my credit card—not because it still smells faintly of urine but because I'm over my credit limit. I stand there staring at her stupidly—doing math in my head—and come to the conclusion that if I ever see that slut lawyer and that illiterate beekeeper again I'll kill them both with my bare hands.

I try my mother's number again. At least my calling card still works. And she's home.

Larry? Are you all right? You sounded terrible in your message. Where are you?

It doesn't matter. If I don't tell you, you won't have to lie—if they ask you. I may be wanted by the police.

What have you done? What's going on?

It's over. He's dead.

Who's dead? Dear God, you haven't gone and *killed* somebody?

No. I haven't done anything. But they're both dead. I'm still not sure who killed who first—but I guess it doesn't matter. It's over.

Take a deep breath, Larry. You're not making any sense.

Sorry. Have you heard from Bonnie?

I'm not sure. *Somebody* keeps sending me these weird faxes.

216

Weird faxes?

Printouts of the names of the graduating class in the Dental Hygiene Department at the B.C. Institute of Technology from 1993—employment records of some dental clinic in Port Alberni.

Unbelievable, I say. And you found the same name on both lists?

How did you guess?

How did I *not* guess for so damn long? Just tell me. Humble or Hamilton?

Hamilton, Artemis. Wasn't she the floozy that crashed Homer's memorial service?

You got it.

What does it mean?

That Bonnie is a hell of a detective. And I'm a damn fool.

The night is hard as the blunt edge of a cleaver. The wind penetrates every stolen sweater and freezes my heart. So what? I pick a direction that feels like west and wave a blue thumb at the blind violence of the traffic.

A long way across this country. Hitchhiking is the ultimate act of faith, I guess. I knew a man, once, who had two stories about hitchhiking—one to explain why he never picked up hitchhikers—the other to explain why he never hitchhiked himself. Both stories sounded like urban legends to me, though he swore they were true. He's dead now, and I no longer doubt his word.

The second story was about a childhood friend of his who set off one spring to hitch to Mexico, sent a single postcard from somewhere in Oklahoma and was never seen or heard from again. Gone without a trace. Family, friends, fiancée—not a word. My friend insisted this was not the kind of guy who would walk away from his life. He just put his faith in the highway—it never brought him back.

The other was a better story. It was about my friend's parents. Touring in their RV one summer they took pity on a hitchhiker somewhere in the desert—a scruffy young character down on his luck. They fed him, encouraged him, befriended him—he accompanied them across many miles of rough country. Finally they parted ways in greener territory, slipped a few dollars in his pocket, and—when he'd insisted on calling it a loan—gave him their home address so he could mail them the money when he got back on his feet.

That's what my friend's parents were like. I only met them once, at his funeral, and I can believe all of this of them. I can also believe that neither of them thought they'd ever hear from their hitchhiker again—but they did. He never did send the money, but he did send a letter confessing that he had been far more desperate than they had imagined when they took pity on him. He had planned to murder them and steal their vehicle—only their kindness had made him change his mind. Thanks to their help he was resolved to turn his life around. He said he was writing to thank them, and also to let them know that he had left behind— under the seat of their RV—the gun he had not shot them with. Sure enough, when my friend's father looked under the seat, the gun was there—a loaded .38.

I told my friend that I'd never have met Bonnie, if I hadn't pulled over for her on that mountain highway. *Besides,* I said, *the whole point of the story is that your parents* did stop, *and the guy* didn't *kill them. Kindness won out. It's a story about* redemption, *about the power of love over fear. If they hadn't stopped, someone else* might *have died.*

My friend just looked at me. *It's okay for you and Bonnie,* he said. *It's okay for my mom and dad. As for me—I don't hitchhike. And I don't pick up hitchhikers.*

He was alone in his truck when he died.

A hell of a big cold country. From here to there. An act of faith, and a surrender. I throw myself on the mercy of the highway and I have lots of time to think—but I try not to. My progress slow and fitful—my life saved again and again by the kindness of strangers—my existence narrowed to a rosary of prayer and travel. Long waits—short rides.

Try not to think. My life, leaving me far behind, like an ocean liner steaming over a distant horizon. The kindness of strangers. Worst are the busy roads—the highway on-ramps near the cities. A mass of terrified humanity, hands gripping wheels, eyes locked on the future, any break in the flow more unlikely than true love.

An elderly woman in a vintage VW takes me to the Sally Ann in Mattawa and buys me an overcoat. A travelling salesman buys me breakfast near Blind River. Near Wawa, I almost die in a blizzard, but a couple of lesbian goat farmers take me home and thaw me in front of a good birch fire—feed me corn bread and goat cheese and too much mead. I crash on their sofa. In the morning the fire is out but the sun streams in and I'm snug under heavy coverlets and I lie there and listen to them making love upstairs. Fresh goat's milk for breakfast, and a ride back to the highway.

I call Adam—once—from a pay phone, but I get his machine, and there is a suspicious humming on the line. I hang up, without leaving a message.

A single ethic takes over my life, arbitrary but essential. *Never refuse a ride.* No matter how short, how uncomfortable, no matter how drunk or scary or malodourous the driver, no matter if the chosen route is not the best or fastest, no matter if the drop-off point is somewhere west of nowhere and you'll have to walk miles before you'll even *see* another car go by. It becomes a point of honour, a superstitious compulsion—taking me nowhere, fast, and sometimes far astray—but necessary. A commitment. A trust. The only one I have left.

I could walk across this country faster, maybe, but that would be too easy. Rather I stand and wait for the impossible kindness of strangers. All I need, now. Near Kakabeka Falls I split firewood for a preacher and his wife. Sink, exhausted, into the fairy-tale softness of the big four-poster bed which used to belong to their daughter, now living in sin in Thunder Bay. They feed me pear pie for breakfast.

Outside Upsala, I wait twelve hours for a ride that takes me less than a mile. In Vermilion Bay, I take a ride with four young Cree guys and two or three days later they drop me off in Oxdrift—about forty-five K's *east* of Vermilion Bay—with a burning joint in one hand, a mickey of gin in the other, a paperback copy of Blake's *Marriage of Heaven and Hell* in my overcoat pocket and the worst hangover I've ever had in my life. They're heading back into Dryden for more beer.

Time to think…time to talk to strangers—telling them nothing. Time to wait. Going nowhere—fast. A gay insurance salesman from Keewatin lets me share his motel room and buys me all the pasta I can eat and never lays a hand on me. I give him the William Blake. Near Neepawa I get a ride with a touring Christian rock and roll band from Sudbury. Snort coke with the lead guitarist in the bus washroom. Never refuse a ride.

On the prairies the rides are more frequent, and even shorter. One day in Saskatchewan I get seventeen rides, travel less than forty miles. Near Foam Lake a guy in a 4 by 4 causes an accident trying to stop for me. Nobody is hurt, but when the screeching and crunching is over four vehicles are damaged—two of them badly—and tempers flare. Two of the drivers end up punching each other in the ditch while the rest of us look on. I wave my thumb at the cars slowing down to get past the wreckage and manage to pick up a lift into Wynard before the cops arrive.

I learn to pray, but my prayers carry no hope of answer or reward. Just a voice in the wilderness—praising the forces that hold me here—acknowledging that this is really where I belong. In Moose Jaw I check the phone book. There are no Secrets.

Never refuse. Beggars can't be. Near Biggar a blonde woman with bad breath and a wandering eye pays me ten bucks to baby-sit her three kids in her trailer while she spends three hours in the bingo hall. Outside Unity I get picked up by a law professor who claims direct descent from Gabriel Dumont, and wants to argue politics. I refuse to disagree with him and he dumps me in Macklin.

Just out of Stettler, on a bright bitter morning, a ten-year-old girl spots me from her living room window and brings me out a steaming mug of cocoa with marshmallows floating on top.

A long long road. Could've made it faster on tortoise-back. An act of faith? *You must be crazy!* How many times have I heard that? The blank, disbelieving stares. *Hitch across Canada in the winter? Must be out of your ever-loving mind...*

Faith. Commitment. A single ethic. Try not to think. Never refuse.

Outside Drumheller, a couple of skinheads try to intimidate me. They want to know if I am a Jew or a communist. I admit that either is possible. I know that if I get in the car with them they will take me into the badlands and dispose of me where no one will find me till I'm as fossilized as all the other dinosaurs. I get in. We end up in Airdrie—drinking beer and watching football in a smoky tavern.

Near Pincher Creek, a beautiful red-haired woman in a Jaguar flashes past me, but I get a ride in the back of a pickup. When they dump me in Fernie—frostbit and nearing terminal hypothermia—there's that Jaguar in a restaurant parking lot. I stagger in and sit at the counter, order coffee and a full breakfast—ham and eggs and sausages and hash browns and flapjacks. No idea how I'm going to pay for it. The driver of the Jag is alone in a corner booth, and she's even better looking when not moving at eighty-five miles-an-hour. When I am warm enough to move without breaking, I approach her.

There is no hint of kindness or even curiosity in the cool blue eyes she turns on me. Excuse me, I say. I find myself a little financially embarrassed at the moment. Don't even have the cash to pay for my breakfast. I was wondering...

You were wondering?

I don't know. If you had any odd jobs I could do for you?

Odd jobs?

You know. Plumbing fixed, firewood split, husband bumped off—that kind of thing?

She laughs, shaking her head. Nothing I can't handle myself, thank you very much, she says, still laughing.

Darn, I say. Maybe they'll let me wash dishes or something.

I saw you hitching back there, she says. I was going too fast to stop. Besides, I don't generally stop for guys who look like they've been sleeping in the ditch. You headed for the coast?

More or less. I take what I can get.

I can take you as far as Yahk, she says. Here—pay for your breakfast with this. It's worth it, just to be able to tell my husband I turned down an offer to assassinate him. He'll be thrilled.

It doesn't take us long to make Yahk. She likes to drive that Jag. I was joking about killing her husband, but by the time I pry my eyes open again in Yahk, I am thinking that might have been more sensible—and safer—than accepting her offer of a lift.

Active faith. Never refuse.

Ride.

Somewhere before Osoyoos I get a lift with an anarchist and his girlfriend and her mother. The girlfriend has a steel bolt through her tongue and she and the anarchist are in the middle of a fight. I get the feeling from the look on the girl's mother's face that the fight has been going on for a while—maybe years—and they only interrupt it long enough to introduce themselves and tell me they are heading for a funeral near Cultus Lake. I sit with the girlfriend's mother—Grace—in the back seat, and we are both wondering if it wouldn't be less painful just to open the door and jump. They feed me bran muffins and soya milk.

Near Sardis I stand for hours before a very familiar maroon Volaré finally wanders off onto the shoulder and waits for me. By the time I get up to it I know it is the same car—but it isn't Art Humbleton behind the wheel—it is Matthew, Margaret's oldest grandson, and he tells me he has driven all the way from Medicine Hat and he feels like a slab of meat and can I drive? He sleeps like a baby. He doesn't even wake up when I have to go through his pockets for cash to pay the ferry.

As soon as I open the front door I know Bonnie is at home. I can smell her. I close the door quietly—the house is dark and silent and full of familiar fragrances—after-images of incense and wood-smoke—a subtle overlay of veggies fried in sesame oil.

My life settling back around me like snow.

Bonnie has rearranged the furniture, again. The strangeness is the most familiar thing of all. But I was mistaken—about the silence. At first I take the distant murmur for a ghost of sound, a memory of last summer's passion, another generation conceived carelessly and with abandon in the bowels of this ghost of a house. But suddenly the voice is clear and present and unmistakable—Bonnie's voice—and it is coming from our bedroom.

At the same moment that I know for sure that it is her, I know also that she is not laughing or crying or singing or whimpering in pain. She is having an orgasm.

Has my life really and truly left me behind, then? For the first time I notice the one thing new in the room—a pair of black rubber boots standing behind the door like they ought to have a farmer in them. Or a bee-keeper.

Bonnie can feel the edge. The lilting panting moaning explosions of her breath—each louder, more desperate than the last. I stand rooted, feeling the house tremble. And then she is over the edge, and each breath is grief and exultation subsiding to a sigh.

The house goes still. I try to close the door quietly. My truck is parked in the street. I wonder if they hear me start it.

It is starting to rain as I pull over to the curb in front of Katherine and Kate's little brown house in Vic West. The Toyota is in the driveway but the house is dark. I remember sitting here like this once before—another night—some lifetime ago it seems. I remember losing my nerve that time—driving off to court other disasters. I have no nerve left to lose. I get out of my truck and ring the bell.

For a long time nothing happens. I ring again and the door swings open and there is Kate, red hair everywhere, barefoot in a lime-green terry-cloth robe, wielding a baseball bat.

Hey—she says. You cut off your hair!

We sit in the kitchen and Kate makes cocoa and Katherine and I eat a whole package of fig bars and I tell them everything. Well— almost. Not all of it is news. When the cocoa is drunk and the last crumbs have been picked out of the corners of the cookie box and I finally complete my tale with a brief description of this evening's events, Katherine shakes her head and says, I wondered where he'd gotten to.

Gotten to?

Your kid brother has been sleeping on our sofa, says Kate. Up until last night. He's working for Kathy at the bookstore.

I thought he was illiterate, I say.

He's very strong, says Katherine.

I knew him immediately, says Katherine. He has that same forth-right endearing arrogance that *all* of you have. He's still got the book—but he won't talk about it. He keeps it in this blue shoulder bag and never lets it out of his sight. He sleeps with it.

What *does* he have to say for himself?

He said he needed a job. Actually, he said he owed *you* money. What could I say? I hired him.

Kate kisses us both and goes to bed. Work in the morning, kids, she says. When she is gone Katherine fills me in on the little she knows. Leila and Duncan have reconciled, of course. Sylvie has moved in with Adam in Vancouver. Bonnie is back to work at Osburn's.

I'm really sorry, Larry, says Katherine. If I'd known he was planning to pull something like that on you, I'd have sent him packing. I always thought you and Bonnie were going to make it.

Me too, I say.

When Y shows up for work in the morning—his blue satchel clamped firmly under his left elbow—Katherine isn't there. He shows no surprise at finding me in Homer's chair, instead. He starts to turn the sign on the door from **CLOSED** to **OPEN**, but I shake my head.

Leave it, I say. We've got to talk.

Y shrugs, takes the bag off his shoulder, places it carefully on the table—sits on it.

You've still got it, I say.

A trust is a trust, Larry. He opens the little leather pouch hanging off his belt and pulls out a slim roll of bills. I'll give you the rest when I get paid Friday, he says.

A trust is a trust?

I'm sorry, Larry. It was Olivia's catharsis. It couldn't be

helped. She had to betray all of us—but mostly she had to betray herself. The law is a disease, Larry, but it's not incurable.

Olivia's catharsis? You use some pretty fancy words for an illiterate bush-boy.

Non-literate, Larry. I got my vocabulary listening to CBC radio. You have a problem with that? Want to hear my Lister Sinclair impression?

No thank you. I want to hear why you slept with my wife.

She's not your wife, Larry. Marriage is a symbolic commitment. Bonnie only commits to *real* things and *real* people, Larry. Besides which—I didn't sleep with her.

I was there last night.

I know. Sometimes being there isn't enough.

What does that mean?

Ask Bonnie.

He meets my eyes absolutely. A trust is a trust. Our father is dead.

Can I see it?

He knows I am talking about the book. No, he says.

Why not?

It's all lies, Larry.

How do you know that?

She read it to me. Until I made her stop.

Olivia?

Yes.

Why did you make her stop?

Why did *you* stop, Larry?

What makes you think I stopped? What makes you think I started, for that matter?

He grins. It was in the book, he says. We read farther than you did. Maybe not all lies…

Maybe not, I say. I don't know. A trust is a trust is a trust, but fiction is just fiction. He's dead—but I guess you know that. Leo's dogs ate him.

His eyes meet mine. Absolutely. For the first time I see he is able to be surprised—shocked—overwhelmed even. It only lasts a micro-second, but in that instant I forgive him. And then—for the first time—he doesn't meet my eyes. Not absolutely, not at all.

We didn't read that far, he says.

But you *knew* he was still alive, I say. You knew it was all faked—that the body on the beach was actually Leo—that the dental X-rays had been switched. What else do you know? Was it *really* cold blooded murder? Or was it self-defense—was all the subterfuge an afterthought? Was it Homer—or was it actually Art Hamilton who killed Leo? Talk about a motive.

Does it matter, Larry? Y gets up and flips the sign on the door. I got debts to pay off, he says.

By the time I get home, Bonnie's gone to work; I guess she's finally back on days. There are two letters stuck through the mail slot. One is a bill from Olivia Astrakhan's office for legal services in the amount of $1139.98. The other is from the Criminal Investigations Department of the Victoria City Police and contains a money order, made out in my name, for $1200.00.

I laugh till I cry.

Bonnie must know I'm here. My truck is back in front of the house; my shoes sit in the very spot Y's boots occupied last night. But she doesn't come into the bedroom until she has had something to eat—I hear the toaster pop—put her work clothes in the laundry hamper and taken a long hot shower. When she finally

228

opens the bedroom door she is naked and steaming, her hair wrapped up in a towel.

Oh, she says. Your hair. Then she laughs and pulls the towel away.

Your hair, I say—stupidly—for her wonderful unruly mass of curls is gone.

I thought I'd lost you, she says.

I thought I'd lost myself, I say.

When I saw your truck was gone this morning—I didn't think you'd be back.

I'm back.

I didn't fuck him.

That's what *he* said, too. I'm glad you've got your stories straight.

I *would* have. Women get horny, too, Larry. He gave me permission—that's all.

I didn't believe him, I say. But I believe you.

We make love for a very long time. Neither of us has an orgasm. For the first time ever this doesn't seem to matter, or maybe it does matter—maybe it matters more than anything. Maybe—at last—it is the real commitment we make to each other. Our need doesn't diminish but it does subside, eventually, into a quiet yearning.

We sleep, still joined.

For the first time in years we have snow at Christmas. It begins falling about ten in the morning on Christmas Eve day and by midnight it is winter. Bonnie and I walk and play in it for hours.

In the morning Leila calls.

I got a bill from Art Humble, she says.

Don't pay it, I say.

Why not?

Art Humble never existed, I say. He was a figment of Homer's imagination.

I *do* pay Olivia's bill. In the end I can't think of anything else to do with money so funny even the cops don't want it.

Y hands me his final pay envelope and asks me to draw him a map to Bone Island.

There's nothing there, I say.

What better place for nobody, he says.

You look like somebody to me.

This is only a body, Larry. Meat. Don't mistake it for a person. I have no identity, I was never legally born—I can't be proven to ever have been anybody. The only name I've got calls everything into question.

What happened in Hollywood?

What do you think happened? They offered us wealth and fame—the usual inducements. It was impossible, of course. No bank in the world will cash a cheque for me, Larry.

It's easy to become somebody, Y.

Exactly. Hard not to. But it's all I've got, Larry. If I was somebody I'd be nobody, but as nobody—I'm really something. Wealth and fame would screw up everything. Olivia couldn't see that. She tried to steal the book.

Homer warned me not to trust her, I say. I should have warned you somehow. Hey, *I'll* take your check, Y. To *me* you are somebody—a brother even—and that's a step down the road, whether you like it or not. We all get to the same place in the end, no matter how often we change our names.

You're right, Larry.

Why not let Homer be dead? He's worked hard enough at it. I bet your mother and your horse miss you like crazy. Keep this money and buy a bus ticket. You can send me the cash when you sell your honey next fall. A trust is a trust.

I've lost two fathers, Larry. You've only lost one.

From what I've heard about Leo, he wasn't much of a loss to anybody.

Only to me, Larry. And since I'm *not* anybody you are right. Leo loved my mother. Homer never did. Homer used her, always, just like he used you and me. Leo never used me.

I'm glad.

Leo was more of a parent to me than Zanzu ever was.

Even after he found out about Homer?

He always knew. He was crazy in love with her and she let some writer she met at some show get her pregnant and then she had the brass to tell him it was his kid. He knew and he never let her know he knew—because he saw that was the only way he wouldn't lose her. As long as she didn't *know* he knew, he had her in his power. *I* was his ace in the hole and he took pretty good care of me. He taught me how to survive—how to be invisible. He never hurt me.

Did you know about the kind of things he did to other people?

I was there when he caught Art Hamilton sneaking in the bushes.

And you knew what he did to him?

I stood in the yard and watched the dogs fight over the scraps.

And you still say he never hurt you?

You have to be somebody to be hurt.

Sorry. I forgot.

Don't trade your power for cheap irony, Larry.

I still don't understand why you want to go to Bone Island.

I have to finish it.

The book?

I learned a lot—looking over Olivia's shoulder. And you're wrong about Bone Island, Larry. There is *something* there. There has to be. It was a dream, and some part of it is here, in this bundle of typing. But Bone Island has secrets, too. It was chosen and modified to be a place of concealment. The cops never found those drug smugglers.

Just their shoes, I say.

At least one of them lived to sell Homer the map. Unless that story is a lie, too. We have only Homer's word, and he was a known liar. What *did* happen to the other smugglers? How did Homer wind up with the pay-off money?

Maybe you're right, I say. Maybe you'll find something there—a hidden door, a secret cave, a mouse-hole in the space-time continuum. Bonnie still swears she saw Homer there one night, you know. He *was* there—I have to believe it now. Maybe if I'd believed it then I'd have been able to dig him out. Maybe it wouldn't have had to end like this.

Don't kid yourself, Larry.

What now?

I have to finish it, Larry.

So I shrug and draw him the best map I can. We're a stubborn bloody bunch, my family. Give my best to Margaret, I say. And here—I push some cash at him—take some food with you.

He laughs, but he won't take the money.

I'm pretty good at taking care of this body, Larry. I've been doing it a while.

I guess you have.

My parents loved me, Larry—all three of them. But none of them had a stinking clue.

In the new year I pick up a couple of little jobs—a basement suite, a sun-deck. It feels very good to strap on my tools and apply the rigors of pure geometry to the recalcitrant material of the real world. I also get paid in full for both jobs—not always a given in this industry.

I don't hear any more from the police, but I do receive an odd clipping in the mail. It comes in a plain envelope, addressed to Loki Thorvaldson, 649 Speed Avenue. No return address, but the postmark looks like Foam Lake, Saskatchewan. The clipping itself is a front page story from the *Pontiac Equity*, about the fire which destroyed the Pontiac House Hotel in Shawville on New Year's Eve. No injuries—but the place burned to the ground. The last paragraph of the story is highlighted:

> Police were unwilling to comment as to the possible cause of the fire except to call the circumstances suspicious. There is speculation that the fire may be connected in some way with a recent incident in which plumbing fixtures were destroyed and a female employee was abducted and sexually assaulted by several as yet unidentified armed men, believed to have been members of a Montreal motorcycle gang.

No word from Y. Winter turns quickly back into grey, and spring comes—audacious and too early and too slow, as always on this rainy coast. Tim finishes Duncan's warehouse, but he isn't invited to the grand opening. Somehow I doubt if *he's* been paid in full.

I'm not invited to the opening either, but I crash it.

I like the haircut, chief, says Duncan—looking around for Leila—blanching only a little.

I see you got rid of that unsightly seismic bracing, I say.

Hey, Larry. Butt-ugly is butt-ugly. I know how to do business in this town. *You* know and *I* know that it would take a nine-point-oh to bring that wall down. If we get a nine-point-oh we'll all be swimming for the far shore together. You've just got to know who to talk to.

Whose ass to kiss, he means, says Leila, joining us at the bar. Glass of wine, Larry?

She gives me a smile so cold and hopeless it breaks my heart. Duncan fills his glass and has the sense to leave us. We wander from the showroom back into the warehouse—already filling with merchandise but cavernous still and full of the echoes of Homer's memorial debacle.

Duncan's agreed to drop all charges related to the concrete incident. With the understanding you won't press the assault.

I know. His lawyer has talked to my lawyer.

I can't believe you're still dealing with that woman.

She's good. And I don't deal with her. She sends me the bill—I pay it.

Does Bonnie know?

Bonnie knows everything.

I'm sorry, Larry. He was ready to nail you to the wall, you

234

know. He had three witnesses lined up to swear you hit him first.

Don't tell me that's why you went back to him—to keep me out of jail. *Please* don't tell me that.

Don't flatter yourself, Larry. You're important to me, but not that important. Maybe if they were going to hang you…

Why, then? You *don't* love him, Leila.

No. But he loves me. Isn't that a hell of a lot better than nothing?

Sylvie has her baby in May, the day after the publication of *Everything but the Truth*. Nobody suggests they name him after his late great-grandfather. The book is reviewed—sometimes kindly—but it doesn't win any prizes and sales are slow. Nonetheless, Katherine calls to ask my permission to try a massive cutting of *Dragons*, the 750 page magic-realist fantasy that Homer spent most of the late seventies and early eighties working on.

It's a horrible job, she says, but I know there's a book in there.

What about your own writing? I ask her.

She shrugs—I can feel her shrug through the phone line. It's up to you, Larry. If you want *that* much for Homer to be dead—you can tell me to stop and I'll stop. Maybe you're right. Maybe there *is* a book in *me*—a better book. Maybe I'm just using Homer as an excuse not to get down to it. I don't know. It's up to you, Larry. You own the copyrights. Tell me what to do.

Sorry, I say. I can't do that for you. Sometimes I can hardly do it for myself.

The earthquake hits one evening while I'm in the bathtub. Just lying there—eyes closed—drifting near the edge of sleep, when everything goes soft and undulates a little and I am wide awake—

eyes open—wondering if this is it—*The Big One*—watching the sway of the shower curtains, the soap jiggling in its dish, the wave patterns. It lasts about fifteen seconds and then it is over.

Not *The Big One*. Not this time. Bonnie calls from work to ask did I feel it?

Leila calls in the morning. Duncan's in the hospital, she says.

What's wrong?

He was working late last night. That wall buckled. Just a little—but a brick fell out and hit him on the head.

Is he all right?

Sure. He's got a hard head, poor dear. They just want to keep an eye on him for twenty-four hours. He's already on the phone to his lawyer to sue the engineer he suck-holed to sign off the revisions to the seismic plan.

I'm glad he's okay.

I almost believe you.

The quake does only minor damage up and down the coast, and Duncan's is one of a handful of minor injuries reported. But when I pick up a newspaper and see the little map with the epicenter marked on it—I get a shiver. Even so, I'm not prepared for the phone call from Margaret.

It's all gone, Larry.

What?

Bone Island. Broke right off like a rotten tooth.

Jesus. Was he still there?

The little brother? If he left he never came our way.

You okay? Your family?

Sure. Take more than a little shaker like that to wash *us* away. But Larry—some things have come ashore.

Things?

Packages. Wrapped in plastic. Most of them are full of money—but one has a whole bundle of typing in it.

Bonnie insists on coming with me to get the manuscript. On the way she insists that we stop at a motel and make love for an hour. Bonnie's getting pretty insistent, these days. We decide we won't open the package till we get home. By the time we get home it is very late.

The book is well wrapped in layers of plastic and duct tape, but sea water has leaked in anyway. I make tea while Bonnie carefully cuts the wrappings and folds them back. The paper inside is soft and mushy with water—blue-grey with the wash of words also gone soft, vague. The whole mess oozes and stinks of kelps and salt and futility.

Compost it, I suggest.

No, says Bonnie. Make a fire in the fireplace, Larry.

It's useless, Bonnie. It's over. It's *mush*—for God's sake.

She leaves the manuscript on the table and takes my teacup away from me and says, *This* is *mush*, Larry. And she kisses me—long slow languid suggestive kisses. Then she stops and looks me in the eyes.

You and Homer put us all through *hell* for that mess of mush. It would poison the compost. Indulge me, Larry. Make a fire—help me dry the damn thing out. If we still can't read it—at least we'll be able to burn it.

Page by page, Bonnie peels away the layers, careful as an archaeologist dissecting the most ancient and sacred text. I crank the fire and get all our extra towels and blankets out of the cupboards and spread them over the fir floorboards and as Bonnie separates the grey, unreadable pages she lays them in careful rows on top of the towels. It is frustrating, painstaking, tedious work, but maybe

237

Bonnie—with her machinist's eye for detail—can discern a text where I see only the shapes and shadows of words, running together, running away.

As Bonnie gets deeper into the pile the damage is less severe, the pages peel apart more easily, are less inclined to collapse into pulp at the slightest touch. But instead of working faster, Bonnie works slower, gazing longer at each page as she spreads it carefully on the terry-cloth—like she's looking into one of those 3-D posters—waiting to get it—knowing she's only got to really relax and just stop *trying* to get it.

I go to bed.

Hours and hours later, Bonnie is there in the bed beside me. The last page is missing, she says.

I know, I say. I *told* you it was useless.

No, she says. Anyway, art is *supposed* to be useless.

Says who?

I don't know. Oscar Wilde, probably. Don't snort, Larry. Anyway, I think Homer probably meant it that way. Nobody ever *really* gets to read the last page, *do* they?

I decide to write to Zanzu about Y. Though I have to tell her they haven't found a body. (Anything can be faked, Larry.) Some weeks later I receive a strange reply. The envelope—postmarked Shawville, Québec—contains a single, creased, grease-grimed sheet of typing paper. When I unfold it I find that it *is* a letter from Zanzu. But the letter is typed—even the signature—and I'd swear every line carries the unmistakable accent of Homer's old Olivetti:

Dear Larry Knee,
I'm very sorry but you must be mistaken. The person
you talk about in your letter can't be my son, as I
have never had any children.
sincerely,
Zanzu Unique

p.s. Here's a strange piece of paper I got from the
plumber who fixed my pump last week. He said he
found it in the wall at the hotel when he was fixing a
broken toilet, before the fire of which you might have
heard. He is French and he couldn't make nothing of
it, but he remembered seeing my name on the paper
and he dug it out of the bottom of his toolbox where
he'd forgot it.